It is time to explore the regions of the Starforce territory.

It's been a while since I wanted to work on the series, after my daughter Meagan was killed, I lost interest in finishing the series, until I remembered that she read the countdown and loved the story and had many questions, In Honor of her I Dedicate this book to her since I wouldn't be writing it if not for her encouragement.

Enjoy reading!

Jeremy

WORLDS UNITE

The Adventures of Starforce book 1

THE RESOLUTE EPOCH

As I began to examine the original storyline, I did not want to tell the readers that Kyle was a royal heir until I started giving hints in the second book. The story seemed useless without the introduction of Prince Kailak. As readers started asking me about Kyle Blake's past, it left me no choice but to explain where he originally came from and how he fits in the story.

Originally, this book was about Starforce as a whole, but after reading some comments of readers, I heeded their advice and added the scene of Kailak and his father, King Savante.

Enjoy reading!

Jeremy

CHAPTER ONE

Prologue

"I will not allow my father to destroy my inheritance. If I do not usurp the throne from him and his court, I will have nothing to rule."

"But then again, by trying to usurp the throne, I put the life of my family as well as my own at risk, I am definitely at a crossroad. Everything depends on my choice. I have some guards that have sided with me, but there are plenty more on his side."

Hearing a knock at his chamber door, his heart began to race. Ziarra's eyes widened, whispering to her husband, "Are you expecting someone?"

Kailak shook his head. Pulling himself together he opened his chamber door, seeing Johan completely out of breath and drenched in sweat. "Please come in Johan."

Johan entered and bowed low in honor of his princess forcing out the words "My Lady."

"What is it? What's wrong?" asked Kailak.

"My Prince, I have word, I overheard some of the king's guards plotting to kill you and your family tonight at midnight."

As he stopped to catch his breath, they both could hear Ziarra sobbing, "It's 7:00pm that is only five hours away from midnight."

"Johan, you've been loyal to me and my family."

"I will fight with you!" Johan exclaimed, interrupting Kailak.

"No! Johan, I could see this day approaching, I have made arrangements with King Lehum of Starforce. He has vowed to hide Ziarra and Kyle until I come for them. Protect them with your life."

"I will not leave your side, until death do us part," sobbed Ziarra.

"You must go! Take our son and keep him safe. One day we will return and rule this kingdom. Johan you know what to do."

Kailak kissed Ziarra and hugged Kyle. "I must go now. I must gather my guards and prepare for battle." Kyle was only two months old. Kailak can't imagine him growing up without a father, but this has to be done, or there will be nowhere safe for them to hide.

"My Prince, I will come back after I get Ziarra and Kyle to Starforce."

Kailak shook his head, "No, this is your only mission now. Do not come back, my life for my son's life."

He nodded and entered the portal to Starforce.

Kailak was not going to die without a fight. He made the bed look as if they were lying under the covers. He had a storage box that he built in the ceiling of his chambers big enough to conceal himself. He wasn't hiding there for long before the guards busted down the door to his chambers. They began destroying things. Pictures were knocked down. Broken glass everywhere on the floor. They blasted the bed destroying it completely.

Kailak remembers when he and Ziarra took the pictures that were being destroyed by the guards; he and Ziarra were out on the courtyard near the purple roses. He could still smell the sweet aroma from the roses as the wind blew through them. Memories of life raced through his mind before having a child. Life seemed simpler, but he would never change anything if he had the chance, he had the family anyone would fantasize about, life was almost perfect.

Kailak wanted to reveal himself and start fighting to protect his chambers, but he knew if he was going to survive, he needed to conceal himself until these guards left.

Kailak heard all the guards leave and so he began to climb out of the ceiling and that is when his father entered, and said, "Hello son, where are your wife and my grandson?"

He dropped to his feet and stood his ground. This is a time when no one stood up against evil on planet Mist, but Kailak will change that. "I will protect my family at all cost even to my death, and my son will return and bring peace back to central Nova."

With those words, his father was angered, drew his sword, and thrust it through his heart, taking his life. As Kailak's breathing slowed down reality started to settle on him as he began to realize that he would never see his family again, but at least they are safe under the protection of Starforce.

Savante felt some pleasure in knowing his throne is safe. The evil intended for his grandson was relieved in killing his own son.

"You just delayed losing the throne. The dream I had was of Kyle taking over the throne, not Kailak." Savante glanced at a familiar voice of his most trusted advisor.

"Mevila, we will not stop looking for Kyle, but he is still only two months old and by the time he is ready to take over my throne, it will be too late."

Mevila motioned for Savante with his hands. "Your Majesty, my son will be assigned to find Kyle when he is old enough. Even though he is only three years old, he will be a great warrior and he is older than Kyle which gives him the advantage."

While King Savante was escorted back to his throne room by Mevila and a few guards, one of his personal guards rushed to Savante's side and bowed. "Your Majesty, our spies have discovered an assassin among our ranks. He was one of Kailak's personal guards."

Before King Savante could react, Mevila replied, "Kailak's personal guards need to be arrested and killed before they revolt. Since Kailak is dead, we need to quench the uprising he started here on planet Mist"

"I agree. Mevila will make the arrangements and I will return to my throne room."

Mevila lowered his head and went to meet with all the guards here on Central Nova.

Mevila first met with Savante's guards. "Our loyal guards, Kailak challenged the leadership of our King, and he was killed and now his guards are still challenging the king's leadership and any traitors will be killed, starting with all of his guards."

Mevila ordered the death of all of Kailak's guards. The day ended in a lot of bloodshed; things are beginning to look bright for King Savante, and dark for the residents on planet Mist. The reign of evil continues on planet Mist with no end at sight.

CHAPTER TWO

Kyle Blake glanced at his partner, "Are you ready?" Joseph popped his neck from side to side causing that annoying sound to crack around his shoulders.

"Yep" Joseph answered,

"Are you going to put on your bullet proof vest today?"

"No!"

Joseph gets annoyed every time Kyle asks that question

"We were called here because an armed, suspicious person killed someone inside this bank, and we need to catch him before he kills anyone else. I really wish you would wear your vest."

"You ask me that before every call out, and we have been partners for eight years. You are like my brother. I have never worn a vest since I have been an officer and I am not starting now."

Kyle heard some commotion inside the bank. He motioned with his hands for Joseph to go around the back and enter from there. He motioned that he would enter through the front.

Joseph went around to the back where he caught a glance of Hellfire escaping. With his gun aimed at Hellfire, Joseph ordered him not to move.

With a quick turn of his head, Hellfire shot two sharp, black darts from his fingers, one striking his hand forcing him to drop his gun, and the other penetrating deep into his chest, knocking him to the ground, allowing Hellfire to escape.

Kyle came out the exact door as Hellfire and noticed his partner on the ground. Running up to him, he said,

"JOSEPH"

Joseph looked up slowly his eyes began to roll behind his eye socket.

"I… am sorry; I have failed. He got away."

Kyle radioed for assistance, "Officer is down, an ambulance will be needed."

He stood up and pointed his gun at Hellfire while he was fleeing and shot off two shots but both missed him as he disappeared into the shadows. He fell to his knees and screamed.

A scream of agony from the depth of his being flowed out of his mouth. He was Kyle's closest friend and only partner, as anger and tears filled his eyes, he was unable to hold it in any longer.

"I will avenge you, my friend." That is when he decided to never take another partner again.

CHAPTER THREE

It has been a few months now, since Joseph was killed by Hellfire, Kyle knew that he would never forget what Hellfire had done, the next time he saw him he would enact his revenge, even though this is his day off. Kyle never really took a true day off. He happened to turn on the television and interrupting the normal schedule, he saw a newscaster explaining:

"This just came in earlier today. Three criminals escaped the maximum security prison in the area. There are no leads as to how they escaped. The authorities have informed us that the names of the three criminals are Mark Tritan, Matthew Fusion, and Peter Xtrobe. The police commissioner, Daniels, has warned everyone in the surrounding area to remain in their homes and keep their doors and windows locked. If you do have to get out, be cautious. The criminals are considered extremely dangerous. It is not yet known if they are armed, we will return to the normal scheduled program."

Colvidre, a city on planet Dextron, Kyle is a detective for the police force on Colvidre. Kyle arrested Matthew Fusion. He was convicted of killing an officer and three other people sentenced for life in the maximum security prison. Mark Tritan killed a man who also helped him experiment on people. Peter Xtrobe an inmate with Mark Tritan, had been an assassin for hire and was arrested by Officer Hotz, a friend of Kyle's.

A dark evening on the streets of Colvidre, the few twinkling lights hung on the residential houses which lit up the streets, but still very dark, you could still feel tension around every corner of the city. Everyone is still uneasy because of the escapees. A man appeared out of a portal and said softly, "I must find Crystal Star before Starforce discovers that we are here, and sends officers to this city to arrest us." "Kahl, stay there I will call on you when I need assistance."

From the other side of the portal a voice growled, "Yes, Master."

This mysterious man is known as the Dark Avenger. He wears a gray and black armor and also wears a helmet which covers his face. A woman passed by and noticed him, as they exchanged eye contact. He started walking towards her. The clanking of his armor made him sound like he was closer to her than he really was. Terrified, she started running away from him not paying attention to where she was going. She turned down a dead-end road.

As he got even closer to her, she started screaming in hopes that someone would come and rescue her. He then called on his servant Kahl. The portal opened, delivering a monster. Then the portal closed, Kahl looked as though he was made from a green slimy jelly. He was a liquid-looking monster. As he walked, he left slimy footprints on the ground.

CHAPTER FOUR

Commander Jurgon a commander of
the police force, arrived on site, "This lady
was slimed by green jelly before she was
murdered? Something does not seem right
here."

"Commander, Kyle is on call today. Do you
think I should call him on this case?" asked
Officer Johnson

"NO!" interrupting in an angry tone,

"Let's get Stevens to investigate this case.
Go look for some evidence while we are
waiting on Stevens to arrive." Jurgon knew
his actions here would have Commissioner
Daniels come down hard on him, but he
was irritated with Kyle and still very jealous
because he wanted to be promoted to
Detective, but Kyle was promoted first.

Commissioner Daniels heard that Jurgon
assigned Detective Stevens to this
case instead of Detective Blake. He called
his secretary. "Jenny, get Commander
Jurgon in my office as soon as possible."

"Commander Jurgon, the commissioner is
requesting you in his office."

Jurgon had been inside the station waiting
on this moment, trying to predict what the
commissioner was going to say and trying

to figure out what his response would be to cover himself. As he entered the office, he asked, "Commander, Detective Blake is on call today, why didn't you call him in on this case?"

Making up an excuse, "I had no other choice; I think Kyle has had a lot on his mind ever since his partner was murdered." As he stopped for a moment a lie came to his mind and he repeated it, "I have heard that he has been using excessive force on most of his cases. That is why he is so good at what he does."

Commissioner Daniels gazed out the window trying to wrap his mind around what he just heard, "Commissioner, I have to go, I still have that report to file before the end of day."

The Commissioner nodded in disbelief as Jurgon left his office.

CHAPTER FIVE

Kahl was getting restless pacing back and forth. "Why is this space craft underneath these streets?"

Dark Avenger replied, "I left it here about three years ago right after I took over planet Mokui to escape the eyes of Starforce while they were joining forces with Mokui."

"I am going to look around and see if I can find Crystal." Kahl was getting impatient waiting inside the space craft.

Dark Avenger answered, "Thanks to our spy who is still inside Starforce. Ten years of searching for the lost heir of planet Mist, our spy informed us that Crystal is searching for the lost heir as well."

Kahl left the space craft in search for Crystal Star. As he was crawling out of a sewer utility access hole, he saw a man sitting near the sewer lid he had just removed. He also noticed another man who looked like a rhinoceros, not too far from the alley on forty-fifth street. Kahl killed the man sitting near the lid and dragged the lifeless body inside a dumpster parked next to the sewer. As he then chased the rhinoceros man away from the area. Then Dark Avenger's voice echoed in his mind, "*Do not leave anything behind.*" So he returned to the area, grabbed the body out of the dumpster, and dragged it down the sewer with him.

"Gather around officers." Called Officer Sanders, "We have just received an emergency call; the caller was real shaken up. She said she saw a monster made up from liquid kill some guy close to the alley on forty-fifth street. Her name is Crystal Gardner. Let us go check it out. The Commissioner said that Kyle Blake will meet us there."

They arrived on forty-fifth street and taped off the area. After they had finished, Detective Blake arrived, walked up to the scene and asked, "what have I missed?' He looked at his old friend, Officer Hotz. He was a very dark skinned man, and he had proven himself very intelligent many times.

"Well sir, we have just arrived here as well. What we do know is that we received a call earlier. The lady, who placed the call, said she saw a monster kill a man here"

Detective Blake looked around the scene. He noticed a dumpster and he continued to look around and saw the alley, it is between two apartment buildings.

"Officer Sanders?" he shouted "Go to those apartments over there and ask the tenants if they saw anything. Also find out what time the dumpster was emptied, and if sanitation picked it up today." He continued, "Officer Hotz, you go with Officer Sanders and find the lady who called earlier."

"Kyle" called Officer Davis, "I found a sewer lid, but I don't see any blood around it."

Kyle crawled inside the dumpster and noticed a very small drop of blood. As he crawled out of the dumpster he replied, "This is very odd, why kill someone and hide inside this dumpster?" He paused, "unless he was hiding from someone, so who was he hiding from and why hide?"

Officer Sanders interrupted him, "Kyle, the dumpster was emptied yesterday, Officer Hotz found Crystal Gardner, and she saw the murder and called it in. She is afraid the monster will return for her."

Kyle turned around, "Officer Young, see if you can get someone from sanitation who also knows about the sewers beneath us and bring him out here, I want to take a team through the sewers to see if there is a trail of blood, Officer Davis, team up with Officer Young and see if they have a map as well for the sewers."

Police Commissioner Daniels is in his office reviewing the report filed by Officer Jurgon, he called to his secretary, "Jenny, get Officer Young in my office."

Jenny picked up the radio and said, "Officer Young, the commissioner needs you in his office."

"Tell the commissioner that I am on my way." He paused for a minute and continued, "Kyle, a man from sanitation will arrive on site in about one hour."

"Thank you, Officer Young. Let's take a break for the next thirty minutes and then everyone let's meet back here"

As Officer Young walked through the police department, a familiar path he had taken more than once, his friend and partner, Officer Jurgon, walked out of his way to stop Officer Young, "The commissioner is going to ask you about Kyle. Make sure you tell him that he has been using excessive force on most of his cases."

He nodded as he walked up to Jenny's desk, "Go on in officer." She told him, "He is waiting on you."

Officer Young gave a usual nod of his head to reveal he had heard Jenny, as he entered the office of Commissioner Daniels "Is it true that Kyle is using excessive force?"

"I've been told that he is using excessive force, but I haven't seen him do it."

"Alright, that is all I need." He waved his hand to let Officer Young know that he could leave the office.

As he left the office, he walked straight up to Officer Jurgon's desk, "There, I said it just like you asked me to."

"Excellent" Jurgon offered with a grin.

"Jenny call in Detective Blake, I need him in my office."

She had seen many things since her first day as the Commissioner's secretary. She gets very nosey when the Commissioner calls in three officers on the same day, "Yes sir."

"Detective Blake, the Commissioner needs to see you in his office."

A voice echoed through the radio, "Okay, Jenny let him know that I am on my way."

CHAPTER SIX

Dalmir, the capital of Dextron, is a city accented with precious zultanite, a greenish grey color stone, the home of Starforce Officers. The King's castle is inlaid with the zultanite stones. Commander Firestar bowed before his King, "Your Majesty, we've discovered that some of our information had leaked out, and the Dark Avenger has discovered that Crystal Star is here on Dextron in the city of Colvidre. He also has learned that she may know the identity of the lost heir to planet Mist."

A King unlike other King's, he doesn't spend a lot of resources on attire. Anyone could still tell he was a King, even with the clothes that he wears, "Firestar, you know as well as anyone that Crystal does not know the identity of the lost heir. Find her before the Dark Avenger does. Have you figured out any information on the whereabouts of Vanisher?"

Prince Derek, a young man in his teenage years. He had not been kept in the castle, but rather spent his spare time learning archery. He was a skilled warrior with a bow, "No, Father, we haven't any new information, but I'm sure he is out there waiting on the Dark Avenger to find

Crystal." "Firestar, good luck on your mission."

Jenny saw Kyle walking towards her. "He is waiting on you Kyle," she said with a smirk on her face-a smirk she gives everyone, a usual expression.

"Kyle, I think you are the greatest detective we have here, but I have had some concerned officers inform me that you have been using excessive force on most of your cases, and I don't need a lawsuit on this department, I have no choice but to take you off this case and the force for a few months with pay while I investigate these accusations. Put your badge and gun on my desk, Detective Stevens will take your place on this case." The commissioner lowered his head ashamed to be put in this situation.

Kyle laid his gun and badge on his desk and left the room to clean his personal desk of his belongings.

Officer Young approached Officer Jurgon while he was at his desk, and slammed his fist on the desk, "I like Kyle, I do not know why you do not like him, but your plan is working. He is leaving. Why did you have to drag me in on this?"

Commander Jurgon, noticeably short with his answers, shrugged his shoulders and looked away.

Kyle returning home to his familiar surroundings, changed clothes wearing a pair of dark blue jeans and a light blue shirt. He sat down to watch a little television after he did a short work out on his weight bench. While he was sitting down, he thought about what happened today. Remembering how Crystal Gardner was terrified that the monster would come and kill her, he decided to go check on her.

Jurgon broke into the investigation room where all the files are kept; he destroyed all the files associated with the murder on Forty-Fifth Street and made it look as though it never took place. On the floor next to the shredded and burnt files, he laid a picture of Kyle that he had found in Kyle's desk, along with a cross necklace identical to the one that Kyle wears.

Kyle stopped his car at the apartments on Forty-Fifth Street and knocked on the door of the apartment number that he got from Officer Hotz earlier today. From the other side of the door he heard a yell, "Who is it?"

"Detective Kyle Blake." "I need to ask you a few more questions about the murder you witnessed near the dumpster earlier this morning."

Crystal opened the door wide enough to look at Kyle, "I am sorry, but a detective already questioned me, and he didn't say he was going to need more information. Now tell me who you really are?"

"Well, I was a Detective earlier today; I was originally assigned to this case. I am Kyle Blake. Can I come in and ask you a few questions?"

Crystal looked at Kyle with curious eyes trying to figure everything out about Kyle, "Yes, but first I would like to know why you are not assigned to this case anymore."

"I was suspended from the force and from this case; they accused me of using excessive force on my cases, Crystal, what exactly did you see earlier?"

Crystal paused for a moment, opened the door, and allowed Kyle in her apartment, "A monster he has the shape of a man, but he looked like a liquid monster, I could see through him. He looked like green slime. His name is Kahl, and he is a criminal, Starforce needs to find out that he is here in Colvidre."

"We are up against a monster?" he paused for a moment, "I'm just an officer here in Colvidre. I don't have any way to contact Starforce." He began to think out loud, "What can I do to bring this monster to justice? The police here will just put the file in an unsolved pile and leave it at that."

"Maybe the police will let you create a super powered team to help them solve these mysteries for them and help Starforce catch criminals and bring them to justice."

Kyle looked at the ground remembering how it felt losing his partner, and how he vowed to never take another partner again in fear of losing them. "That is a good idea Crystal, but I don't think the police would let me, and even if they did, I don't think I could allow anyone to get hurt because of me, and Starforce is not really allowed in this city." Kyle handed her his card "Here is my card. Call me if you think of anything else that might help the case." He left her apartment.

Officer Hotz was returning a file to the investigation room. As he opened the door, he noticed it had been broken into and that there were burnt papers scattered all over the floor, "Get the Commissioner in the file room now! Someone broke into it" He pointed to another Officer, "Officer, you go get Detective Watkins in here as well."

CHAPTER SEVEN

As Crystal was taking a stroll outside her apartment. Out looking for some evidence the police may have missed, she noticed someone sitting near the dumpster. He looked as if he had not showered in weeks. His skin was a grayish color, as she started walking closer to him in her investigation of him, she immediately noticed he had a horn on his forehead, and that he was a rhinoceros man. His clothes were ripped and he had holes in his jeans. Crystal had seen many exotic aliens in her lifetime so his appearance didn't bother her, "Are you an alien?"

His first reaction was to raise his hands and show he was harmless, "It's okay. Please do not scream."

"Do you know that a murder had taken place here?"

"Yes ma'am, I saw the whole thing and the liquid monster chased me away trying to kill me as well."

Crystal looked deep into his eyes and she could tell almost immediately that he was harmless, and had no intention of hurting her, "What is your name?"

"David Stanley, but my friends all call me Rhino, what is your name?"

Crystal extended her hand to shake, "I'm Crystal, and it's nice to meet you. You know, I have a friend who would like to meet you as well and ask you a few more questions about what you saw here. Come to my apartment where it is safe."

Crystal led the way as Rhino followed her, "It's not much further" she assured him

"Are you sure you want me inside your house? I look like a monster and we have just met, I can wait outside"

"No sir, you can come inside and take a shower as well, I will see if I can find you some clean clothes that will fit you"

"You are the nicest person that I have met in a long time, I can't remember too much of my past life." He looked towards the ground like he was ashamed or hurt since he was unable to remember that far into the past"

"It's okay now, we are here." She opened the door and allowed him inside, "You can take a shower while we wait for him. There are towels in the right side of the cabinet underneath the sink. Make yourself at home."

As Rhino showered Crystal called Kyle, "Hello, Kyle, this is Crystal. Something came up and I need you to come over and bring an extra-large pair of jeans and a shirt, I found another witness, I will explain everything else when you arrive."

"Alright, I'm on my way." Kyle hung up the phone.

Detective Watkins did a visual scan of the investigation room, "It looks like Kyle did this, I found a picture of him and the necklace that he wears on the floor over there." He pointed towards the burnt pile of files, "I have not found any fingerprints yet, so I could be wrong. By my initial examination of the room, I think someone is trying to make it look like Kyle did this."

"But who would have done such a thing? I am sure he did this, but he wanted us to think that he was framed; we need to get a warrant, Officer Young you go get the warrant."

"Okay, Commander Jurgon."

It was a newly familiar site for Kyle as he pulled into a parking space right outside of

Crystal's apartment. She lives on the second floor of the expensive apartment complex in the city of Colvidre. It reminds Kyle of a condominium. A security guard walked past Kyle as they exchanged eye contact. There is an instinct in any police officer that they can recognize another officer even off duty. It is how they carry themselves. As he stood in front of Crystal's apartment door, he contemplated what he would do if Crystal was in trouble inside and that this could be a trap. He clinched his fist and knocked on the door. He heard movement inside the apartment. He was relieved when Crystal opened the door.

"This is the strangest thing I have ever been asked to do."

Crystal grabbed the clothes from Kyle, "Come inside have a seat, I will explain more when I return."

She laid the clothes down by the bathroom door, "Here is some clothes. Try them on and see if they fit you." She called to David, as she was walking away from the bathroom door. Returning to her living room, she could hear Rhino reply

"Okay, thank you."

Crystal sat on her couch, "I was reviewing the murder scene today, when I noticed a guy sitting by the dumpster. He also told me that he saw the monster as well, but then it chased him away from the area. He does not have a place to stay. Could we at least find him a place to stay to repay him for his help?"

"Wow the clothes fit me." He noticed Kyle sitting on the couch and replied, "Thank you for the clothes."

Kyle had seen many strange aliens in his life, but he never saw one that looked like a Rhinoceros. He stood up to be polite and extended his hand, "My name is Kyle Blake."

"I'm David Stanley, but everyone knows me as Rhino, Crystal thank you for letting me shower."

"Until we get you a place to stay of your own, you can stay at my house. I have some questions about the murder you witnessed."

As Rhino sat down on a chair, Kyle continued, "Did you see where the monster came from?"

"Yes, he came out of a sewer lid; it made so much noise I am not sure how no one else heard him exit the sewer."

Officer Young walked up to Commander Jurgon's desk, "I have the warrant. Let's go bring Kyle in to question him."

"Thank you, my friend." They started walking to their police cruiser.

CHAPTER EIGHT

Dark Avenger looked around, "It was a great idea to open a portal four years ago in the sewer here on Colvidre. My space craft is undetectable down here."

"Too bad that we are leaving it down here. We really should take it back with us when we are finished here."

"Kahl, do not forget what we have come here for. We must find Crystal before Starforce finds her. She suspects the royal heir to be here on Colvidre. If Starforce finds him before we do, they will groom him to take his rightful place on planet Mist."

As Kahl was leaving the space craft he added, "If Vortex was right and Crystal does know that the royal heir is in this city, it will not be long before Starforce shows up. I will go back up and look for her again"

"No, Kahl, let's give Starforce some time to show us where she is. Then we will capture her and get the information about the royal heir."

Kyle looks around Crystal's apartment, "Thank you for the answers, Rhino. I need to go finish some unfinished business with the police. You stay here with Crystal and protect her. I will be back to pick you up."

Kyle stood up and started walking towards the door, Crystal followed right behind him, "Bye Kyle. Do not be long, it is not safe."

As Kyle was getting in his car he replied, "I will be back as soon as I can, please stay inside your apartment, and let Rhino protect you. He will keep you safe." Kyle had not felt an emotional connection with anyone since his partner was murdered, until now. Kyle thought as he was driving, *"Could I have found my future wife? I have never wanted to protect someone so sincere."*

Commander Jurgon motioned for Officer Young to kick the door open to Kyle's house. With a crash the door broke from the hinges. Commander Jurgon allowed the other Officer's to enter ahead of him. Since Kyle was not home, they began to look through his things to see if they could find evidence against him.

"Kyle is not here Commander. There is no evidence to explain why he wanted to break into the file room and burn the files there."

"Well maybe he went to the station to pretend nothing had happened. Let us return to the office now and he will come to us." Commander Jurgon knew that since Kyle did not break into the investigation room, and that he would return to the station to find out what was going on. Jurgon was planning a trap for him there. No Officers stayed behind they all returned to their cruisers and returned to the police station.

Anger consumed Kyle's thoughts as he arrived at his house and noticed the front door kicked open. As a detective he examines the scene and realizes that the police had done this, *"What could the police have wanted here?"* He sat down and got himself calm and called the station, "Jenny, I need to speak to Commissioner Daniels."

"Commissioner Daniels speaking, how can I help you?" Kyle replied, "Why did you guys break in my front door? What were you looking for?" Commissioner Daniels motioned for Jenny to start recording the conversation. Commander Jurgon entered the office and whispered, "Is it Kyle?" He nodded, "Kyle, I am not sure what you are talking about, but I will send a few men over. Are you at home?" Kyle said, "Yes, I am home." He hung the phone up and took a few small breaths to relax and calm down from all the anger he was feeling. He knew it was not the Commissioner's fault.

"Kyle is home, go bring him in. Take a few men with you, except Officer Hotz. He had to go home unexpectedly due to some personal problems, he is dealing with a lot at the moment." Jurgon nodded and went to gather a team of officers together.

Chapter Nine

"If the police didn't break into my house, then I wonder who did. I think there is more going on at the station than I am aware of."

A portal opened up in the middle of Kyle's living room and a man with a star on his chest appeared out of the portal, "Greetings Kyle Blake, I mean you no harm. I am from Dalmir. My name is Commander Firestar. I am a Starforce officer. Where is Crystal Gardner? She is here on Colvidre on a mission, and I know that you know where she is. We have little time before the Dark Avenger and his servant Kahl find her. I must find her before they do."

Starforce officers usually do not come to Colvidre since we have law enforcement here, unless it is something major, Kyle remembered when a riot broke out here, the police were not able to calm the riot. Starforce officers showed up and the riot ceased immediately. They heard police sirens getting close, "The police are on their way here."

"They will only slow us down; there is something bigger here than they are prepared to handle, Kyle, hold on to me we will run past them."

Kyle looked at Firestar with a very puzzled face. In his mind he was thinking, *"I hope you know what you are doing."*

He grabbed hold of Firestar, "Crystal lives on Forty-Fifth Street."

Firestar started running going faster with every step he took, until he was a blur to anyone standing by watching. He threw a karate star unlike any karate star that Kyle had seen before. The star hit the tire on the driver side of the police car, stopping the car instantly.

Officer Young got out of his car, "What was that? Whatever it was it hit my tire."

Commander Jurgon pushed the front door open and replied, "Kyle, come out with your hands up."

"It looks like he is gone again, Commander."

Dark Avenger stopped in his tracks, "Do you feel that Kahl?"

"No master, what do you feel?"

With a disappointed reaction Dark Avenger replied, "Firestar is here, I can sense him. That means the rest of his Starforce unit will be here soon."

"We cannot fight them without an army. There are too many of them."

Dark Avenger laughed, "We will have to find another way, and we might have to change our plan." He walked around part of the space craft with his hands folded behind his back as he was thinking, "Kahl go look for Crystal one more time and also look for Firestar, this time put on your armor suit, since you haven't worn it since we have been looking for Crystal."

Kahl nodded for he only had one armor suit that hid his hideous form from everyone, making him look like a normal person.

Kyle knocked on Crystal's apartment door. She opened the door with a shocked face as she saw Firestar standing at her door, "Firestar, what are you doing here?"

"This situation has just gotten more serious. Dark Avenger and Kahl have figured out that you are here on Colvidre, and they also believe you have found the lost heir, King Melach, Prince Derek, and your son Northstar, are worried for your safety. They sent me here to find you and protect you, I will contact Starforce so I can let them know you are safe and we are not too late."

"How is Nathan involved?" It had been a little over five years since she had seen her son. She had been searching for the heir to the throne of mist and her search has brought her to Colvidre.

Firestar's face glowed as he explained, "Nathan is a mighty Starforce officer. He is more skilled than you or I. He went on a mission with Commander Jacen and he killed King Savante and Mevila and now Dark Avenger is after you. We believe that he wants to kidnap you and ransom you off, so that he can get revenge on Nathan, also known as Northstar, that is what our spies have told us."

Crystal remembers a time when she loved the man called Dark Avenger. He was a

Starforce officer, his name was Spartan. No one knows that Spartan and Dark Avenger are the same person except Crystal and Firestar. Northstar has no idea that his father is Spartan.

Kyle interrupts, "Crystal you are from Starforce?"

"Yes, I was assigned to secretly find the missing heir to the throne of Mist."

Firestar presses his communicator, "Starforce send my team to my location here on Colvidre."

"They have been waiting on you Commander." Suddenly, a portal opened up and three men stepped out of the portal.

"My name, as you already know is, Firestar, I can run faster than the speed of light."

He is almost bald except for a long, white, bushy ponytail on the top of his head. He pointed to the first guy that came out of the portal.

Kyle interrupted, "Maverick, I didn't know you joined Starforce."

"Kyle Blake, it has been about twenty years. Yes, I was recruited by King Melach when he arrived on Colvidre to find his wife."

Firestar added, "Maverick created the armor that he wears. It gives him the ability to fly, and it also enhances his physical abilities. He created some of the newer, high technical weapons, like the small pocket bomb, a freeze ray, a flamethrower, and a heat seeking arrow to shoot from a bow."

As Kyle examined Maverick's armor, it was very shiny and clean. It showed his ability to create whatever he could think of.

Firestar pointed at another Starforce officer. He is skinny, five'4 tall, and has short black hair, very clean cut, "This is Dexter. He is a martial arts master on his home planet, and he can stretch his body parts to his advantage to overcome an opponent."

"This is Grant, and he is here to protect you Crystal. Not much is known about him, since he arrived on Dalmir at a very young age. He can move with a thought. His powers are still very mysterious. This is my Starforce unit."

Kyle introduced himself, "I am Kyle Blake, I am an officer of the police here on Colvidre. When I was younger, I earned the nickname Shockwave. This is Rhino"

"Rhino and I saw Kahl kill a man in the alley right outside by the dumpster. He never saw me, but he did chase Rhino away from the scene," Crystal retorted.

As Commander Jurgon was walking to the commissioner's office, he saw him through the glass walls and replied, "Come in Commander Jurgon."

Commander Jurgon replied, "Kyle wasn't home, but we could tell that he had been there prior to our arrival."

"All we can do now is wait. While we are waiting, I will have every police unit be on alert and have them keep an eye out for him as well. They will bring him in if they spot him."

As Jurgon left the office he thought, *"This is working better than even I had planned. If*

*Kyle keeps hiding, it will make him look even
more suspicious."*

Firestar pressed his communicator.
"Starforce, this is Commander Firestar. I am
going to need the freeze ray to help bring
the Dark Avenger and Kahl back with us.
I've got a strong feeling that it is not going
to be an easy task."

His Communicator started blinking,
"Firestar, this is Venus. It will take me about
an hour or so to get it for you, as soon as I
get it. I will teleport it to you on Colvidre,
Northstar is asking about his mother. Is she
okay? Did we get to her before the Dark
Avenger?"

"Yes, we got to her before the Dark Avenger
or Kahl got to her. She is coming back with
us to Dalmir."

Kyle began to feel a little crowded. He said,
"I need to talk to the police and find out
why they broke into my house, and what
they were looking for. I will be back here in
about an hour if not sooner. If I am not

back, go without me and I will join you as soon as I get a chance."

"We will arrive at the police department to get you, if you're not back here in about an hour." Rhino retorted.

Kyle agreed, "Firestar, can you give me a ride back home?"

"Yes, but you will have to hang on."

As they left the apartment, Firestar started running. Before he reached the end of the apartment, he was running so fast it was like a blur.

Detective Watkins opened the commissioner's door and closed the door behind him, "Sir, I had the necklace examined for prints, and the prints found do not belong to Kyle. They are from commander Jurgon. I believe he is trying to frame Kyle and get him kicked off the force. With your permission I'd like to question a few officers before I pursue that thought too far."

With a nod he answered, "If you see Kyle, bring him to my office to see me, I want to give him a heads up on what is going on here."

As Detective Watkins was leaving, he added, "I do not think he will come back for a while, but if I see him, I will escort him here."

After stopping at his house Kyle remained very still, allowing his vertigo to stop spinning, he said, "Thank you for the ride."

"You're welcome." Firestar continued his sprint back towards Crystal's apartment.

CHAPTER TEN

Dark Avenger saw Kahl returning from outside the space craft, "Did anyone see you?"

"I think Firestar spotted me and I was unable to find Crystal, Starforce must have found her already."

With a jerk of his head he replied, "Firestar saw you? We had better prepare for battle then, I am going to use the flame thrower that we stole from Starforce, I am pretty sure that Firestar will try and use the freeze ray to capture us, but we will surprise them this time."

Kahl bowed as he left to go get the flame thrower just as Dark Avenger had ordered. It led him to the cargo area on the space craft which was on the lower level of the craft. As he landed his foot firm on the last step, he heard, "Psst!"

Kahl jeered his head to the prison cell and saw a short, green, goblin alien, "I forgot that we put you in the cell after we conquered planet Mokui."

"Get me out of here! I promise to be good."

Kahl began to ignore the small goblin alien and continued to retrieve the flame thrower. He heard the alien scream, "WHEN I GET OUT OF HERE, I WILL ENACT MY REVENGE ON YOU, AND THE DARK AVENGER." Kahl grabbed the flame thrower and started back up the stairs.

Kyle arrived at a familiar building. Colvidre Police Department, a gray brick building with large glass windows around the entrance. As he walked through the front doors, Officer Young saw him. "Kyle, I have a warrant for your arrest."

"Officer Young I have worked alongside you for the last three years; I am here to see the commissioner. You can follow me to his office if you'd like."

Detective Watkins walked past and noticed the two arguing, "Officer Young, I will handle this, Kyle, the Commissioner is waiting on you in his office, I will escort you."

As they walked towards the commissioner's office, down a hallway that Kyle had walked down many times before, Detective

Watkins broke the silence, and said, "Kyle, we have an officer, that I believe is trying to frame you."

Kyle answered, "Commander Jurgon has been trying to get officers against me. He is a good commander and an asset to this force. But only if this force acts like a team, and only then will we succeed at what we do."

Commissioner Daniels saw Kyle through his glass door and motioned for him to enter, "Kyle, I am glad you stopped by. Please have a seat. I need to talk to you."

Kyle sat down on the hard cushion chair that was in front of the desk. He thought, *"this is the chair no officer wanted to sit on. It is like sitting on a rock-very uncomfortable."*

"Kyle, we went to your house to search for some evidence because we thought that you broke into the investigation room the other night. But we were wrong. Another officer had done it and he made it look as if it were you. He left a picture of you and your necklace was lying on the floor."

"I'm wearing my necklace sir." He showed the Commissioner the necklace still around his neck, Commissioner Daniels replied, "I am sorry for any damage that occurred. We will pay you for any damage. We are arresting Jurgon as we speak. That is all. You may go and if you want, you can come back to work tomorrow, or take a few more days off with pay."

"I will be back tomorrow and then we can talk more."

As Kyle left the office, Watkins entered. "Sir, Officer Young was the only officer that knew about Jurgon breaking into the investigation room. He was threatened by Jurgon. I am personally going to arrest Jurgon."

Commissioner Daniels nodded, "Go bring him to my office so we can talk to him."

Firestar arrived at Crystal's apartment, which was not the best-looking apartment complex in an incredibly good neighborhood here on Colvidre. He thought, *"She is under cover well. Not even the Dark Avenger would have looked for her here. With the resources of Starforce behind her, she could have gotten a very nice house or even a larger apartment. That was weird seeing that armor earlier, I remember coming to Colvidre to get Maverick to help Starforce, and how Maverick had lost his family at the hands of a mad man who stole a weapon the Maverick had created for the government here on Colvidre."*

He knew that Maverick had created a lot of armor and weapons for both Starforce and Colvidre. As he entered the apartment, he said, "I saw this man in armor that I recognized from somewhere and now I think I remember, that armor had been worn by Kahl when he was first mutated into the liquid monster that he is now, The Dark Avenger and Kahl are in the sewers right underneath this apartment complex."

CHAPTER ELEVEN

Firestar remembered when Dark Avenger and Kahl were both Starforce officers. He also remembered that Dark Avenger and Crystal had once loved each other, Dark Avenger arrived at Starforce young from planet Mist. He wondered if there was any good still inside him or if he was under the influence of another person sent to infiltrate Starforce from within. His communicator started beeping, "Firestar, this is Venus. I am teleporting the freeze ray now."

He held out his hands with his palms up and the freeze ray appeared in his hands, "Thank you, Venus." He replied as he pressed his communicator.

"Now let's go get them while we have the upper hand." Rhino interrupted Maverick. "Not yet, we need to wait for Kyle to get back."

Upon hearing the conversation, Kyle walked up to the apartment, "I am here. Do we know where they are hiding?"

"They are hiding in the sewer." Kyle nodded at Dexter and replied, "There is a lid to the sewer right outside this apartment complex."

Commander Jurgon entered the brown, tinted, brick building known as the Colvidre police department. The two glass entry doors closed behind him as he started down the stairs to his office. Being stopped by Detective Watkins, "Commander Jurgon, you are under arrest for breaking and entering into the investigation room and destroying police property."

"I did not do it. You know it was Kyle."

"Jurgon, you can stop the pretending. We have your prints on the necklace. Kyle still thinks you are a good man. So, you may want to put these childish actions behind you and grow up, I genuinely think you can be an asset to this department, if you stop trying to hurt us."

Knowing that Detective Watkins was right about what he was saying Jurgon replied, "The hatred that I have displayed towards Kyle is wrong. With all that I have done to him, he still thinks that I am a good person inside. I don't understand, I will learn to do what is right."

To avoid any embarrassment, Watkins did not place handcuffs around Jurgon's hands. They both walked to the Commissioner's office.

Kyle led Starforce to the sewer lid. Looking around he said, "Rhino you will have to open the lid. It is very heavy."

Rhino pulled the lid off the sewer opening, giving a small grunt. Laying the lid to the side, he moved out of the way. Kyle glanced down the ladder and saw a trail of blood spots on the edge of the sewer ledge. "I wonder if Kahl left these blood spots on purpose to lead us to them."

Firestar, Grant, Maverick, Dexter, Crystal, and Rhino followed Kyle down the ladder to the ledge where the trail of blood started. As they followed the trail, Firestar turned around to the rest of the team, "We need to be quick and keep our voices down. They could be anywhere."

As they turned down a corner, they stopped in their tracks. There was a very gigantic hole in the bottom of the sewer floor. As they walked close to the edge of the hole, looking down, Firestar said, "It's too dark to see the bottom of the hole, Maverick fly down that hole a little ways down and see if you can see anything there."

As Maverick hovered down the hole, his jet pack lit the way down as he floated downwards. The farther down the hole he got the lighter it got. He noticed that there was light at the bottom of the hole. He landed on the bottom of the hole and stood in awe. His view consisted of a space craft at the bottom of the hole. It made him wonder how the space craft got down there, and when did it get there, without Starforce knowing about it. He thought, *"We must have a traitor inside Starforce to be able to hide this from Starforce."*

Maverick flew full power back up to the top of the hole. "Firestar, there is a space craft at the bottom. It looks as though it appeared out of a portal and fell to its rest at the bottom."

Maverick carried everyone down the hole, one at a time. Rhino got to the bottom and noticed the floor was not moist, but was dry. Looking at the walls around them, were dry as well. It doesn't look like a sewer because it's so dry. The air is also dry. No moisture is in the air. The air smells fresh, no raw sewage smell.

"If the Dark Avenger is inside this space craft, then let's not keep him waiting on us." Grant said, as he stared in awe of the v shaped craft. Firestar led the team inside the space craft.

As they entered the loading dock, they had a glance of the Dark Avenger waiting in the bridge of the craft, "About time you arrived, Firestar. I am disappointed in you I expected you sooner."

Grant replied to the Dark Avenger, "You can just give up now; you can't destroy all of us."

With a sinister laugh he replied, "Maybe I cannot, but it will not stop me from trying. Kahl, attack Starforce."

Kahl appeared from the shadows and launched himself at Grant as he dodged Kahl, Dexter stretched his leg and kicked

Kahl. As he did, it knocked him backwards to the floor, Grant shot off a blast of electricity at Kahl, making him hit the ground hard with such a force it slid him across the floor and knocked the breath out of him. His body became numb due to the electricity still flowing through his body.

Dark Avenger took this moment as half of Starforce was fighting Kahl, "I have been looking for you Crystal for about five years now, and I have finally found you. You will not escape me."

Crystal ran up to Dark Avenger ready to kick him in the chest, but he forced a blast out of his fists at her, hitting her with enough force to knock her up against the entrance door, Kyle saw it happen, but his response was too late. He ran up to Dark Avenger and began to initiate a fist fight, but to no avail. He continued to block every punch or kick that Kyle threw at him, as if he seemed to be saving his energy for the right time.

As the feeling returned to Kahl's arms and legs, he blasted himself to Dexter biting his arm. Dexter screamed in agony as the pain surged through his body. Seeing everything going on, Firestar pointed the freeze ray at Kahl, and when Dexter broke free of Kahl, Firestar blasted the freeze ray at him, freezing him solid.

Dark Avenger was bored with Kyle and said, "Enough!" He hit Kyle so hard it lifted him off the ground. He soared through the air and hit the far wall. Looking at the freeze ray he replied, "Firestar I came prepared this time. I predicted you would bring the freeze ray."

Grabbing the flamethrower, he fired the flames at Firestar. As he began to outrun the flames, he threw a few karate stars at the Dark Avenger. Still in a lot of pain, he was losing blood but with all his might that was left, Dexter stretched his leg and kicked the flamethrower out of his hands.

Maverick flew up in the air. Firestar grabbed the freeze ray and threw it at Maverick, Dark Avenger dashed to pick the flamethrower back up, Maverick landed behind him and in a desperate attempt, the Dark Avenger grabbed the flamethrower, and before he could turn around, Maverick fired the freeze ray at the Dark Avenger turning him into a block of ice.

Firestar ran up to Dexter and offering sympathy. He said, "Are you okay?" he nodded, "I will be fine. It is just a bite. I will need to get it treated though."

Firestar pressed his communicator. "This is Firestar. We have the Dark Avenger and Kahl on ice. Teleport them to Starforce headquarters. Dexter is hurt and needs medical attention, and I will be there soon."

Kyle glanced around at all his new friends and said, "Thank you for all of your help. I hate to see you guys leave, but you have your own city to protect."

Crystal glanced at Kyle with an innocent look and replied, "I will be back, I promise you."

"Crystal, you're leaving as well?" Kyle replied disappointed.

"It is okay. Kyle, I must go. It is my home and I miss my son and want to see him; I also need to check in with my King, but I will be back."

A portal opened and swallowed Dark Avenger and Kahl as it closed.

Maverick said, "I am going to stay here a little while longer. There are things in my past that I must face."

Firestar nodded, "I know Maverick, and don't forget to finish your original mission. We will be back."

They entered the portal and disappeared.

CHAPTER TWELVE

The sun began to rise as another day was beginning. Kyle had returned to the Colvidre PD. As he walked by the commissioner's office, he heard a familiar voice. "Kyle, we have an emergency that I need you to check on. A gentleman called the emergency call center. He said that he and his family are being held hostage inside his own house. The man said he recognized his captor as Matthew Fusion, who also escaped prison with Mark Tritan."

"What is his name and address, and I will check it out?"

"His name is Kevin Fitzwater and his address is 542 Southwest Union Boulevard." He added, "Kyle, I have to get this approved first but, I want you to lead a special task force here on Colvidre, I will give you the choice of your companions. I will make this announcement as soon as Starforce approves it."

"Look there!" Officer Sanders pointed to a window as Matthew Fusion walked past it, "He is heading to the north side of the house."

Kyle pulled up next to him and he looked around doing a visual scan of the house and the surrounding area. Detective Watkins walked up next to Kyle, "He has not made any demands yet. We have tried to make contact, but he refuses to comply."

"Where is he inside the house?"

"We spotted him heading to the north side of the house from that window." Officer Young pointed to the window.

Kyle answered, "We need to find out which side of the house the family is being held captive and find out which part of the house the captor's at."

Officer Young picking up his radio said, "Twenty-seven to headquarters."

A voice echoed through the radio, "Go ahead Twenty-seven."

"We need a sniper over here. Send us Thomas Riley. We need to see if we can locate the family and Matthew Fusion inside the house."

Suddenly Kyle noticed a lot of commotion between the other officers. Officer Sanders pointed to the same window. "There he is!"

Immediately Kyle shot his firearm as he pointed it at Matthew Fusions head, killing him instantly. Officer Young spoke up, "Kyle, why did you kill him?"

"If I didn't shoot him, he would have killed the family inside the house."

Officer Young questioned his reasoning. "How do you know? He may have wanted to surrender."

Kyle pointed to the side of the house, "See that antenna? That is a scanner antenna, and if the scanner is tuned into our frequency, he just heard that we called for a sniper and that is how I know that he would have killed the family, and that is also why he moved close to the window."

Detective Watkins noted, "Good job Kyle. I did not even notice the antenna."

"Detective Watkins, take charge here. I am going back to the PD. Give me a call if you need me or if the medical examiner needs me."

INSURRECTION

CHAPTER THIRTEEN

Special Task Force

A normal day as Officer Hotz, being a tall Black officer, he is feared by many since he has a gruff voice, but today he looks very rough in his appearance, he walked in the Police Station, having the last two days off, being in a hurry, he passed all the commotion in the lobby. Heading straight to the commissioner's office

He was expected 10 minutes earlier, running behind he is rarely late for anything, but today he is in distress since his son has been missing for over a day, and his phone goes straight to the voice mail, "Commissioner, my son has been missing for over twenty-four hours, I have looked everywhere he hangs out at, I need help. Can we get a search team to assist me in the search?"

A noble request for a valued officer, knowing the lengths any man would go to find a child the commissioner answered, "As a fellow member of this Police department, you have every right to get assistance in this matter. Let me get the paperwork ready, please have a seat."

Many things began to run through the mind of the Commissioner he thought to himself, *"This is a great officer, and the department can't afford to lose his experience and stature, I wished there's a way to prevent these things from happening to good people."*

The commissioner asked a question on the paperwork, "Do you know who could have taken your son?"

Trying to hold back his tears the pain of losing a child is unbearable, as anger began to rise-up within himself, he replied, "IT WAS MARK TRITAN." Trying to calm himself down because he realized he began to yell; he began to slow his breathing down so he could remain calm. He continued, "He just escaped, and he threatened me when I arrested him, told me he would have his revenge on me."

"This is tragic, but I have the perfect Officer to assist you." Seeing Kyle walking towards the officer he continued, "And here he comes."

Commissioner Daniels motioned Kyle to come in and he replied, "Detective Blake, I have your first assignment as a special task force leader. Assist Officer James Hotz as he looks for his son, he has been missing for over twenty-four hours; he believes Mark Tritan kidnapped him, get your team ready."

Kyle glanced at Officer Hotz and his expression shows how deeply concerned and how much regret he is going through because his son is missing, "James I have to go get my team together, go home and get a recent picture of your son, and let's meet back here in fifteen minutes."

Officer Hotz nodded and did not say a word since he knew if he tried to say anything, he would break down in tears.

They both left the commissioner's office, Commissioner Daniels thought how Kyle was the greatest detective he had known, "*I am sorry to lose you in this field, but I know you will be just as good as a leader, as you were a detective.*"

Maverick looked at Rhino and said, "I use to live in this city not too long ago, I think

Dalmir is a beautiful place to live, and I have been on many planets, I use to work for a weapons manufacturer here on Dextron, I was the weapons engineer. I created all kinds of secret weapons for the company, until one of my weapons was stolen by a mad man who was also employed with the same company, and he killed my family with the weapon, and he happened to get away with the crime."

Before he could finish his conversation, Kyle walked in the room and said, "We have a case; let us get ready. We have to find a teenager who was possibly kidnapped, we are to meet his father and fellow officer at the police station in about ten minutes."

Memories of his own family began to flash before Maverick's eyes knowing how losing a child affects a person, even though the child is a teenager, he replied, "It's not an exciting case, but most likely a more important case then an exciting case."

Kyle answered, "Maverick you are so right, his father and I are good friends. And I don't want anything to happen to this kid."

Rhino exclaimed, "We need to get on the move if we want to find this teenager."

Maverick agreed, "I am just use to being a Starforce officer and taking on big cases."

"But these are some of the cases we get here on Colvidre, we are not Starforce officers, so our cases are what are assigned to us."

Maverick agreed with Kyle, "You are right. Should I wear my armor?"

Kyle replied, "No, not yet. Let us work up to that, until then let us wear police uniforms." He handed the uniforms to the guys.

As they entered the Police station Kyle pointed to the break room for employees, "Maverick, you and Rhino hang out in the break room, I am going to go meet up with the commissioner for a minute and I will be back."

Rhino raised an eyebrow to Kyle and said in a joking tone, "Sure thing, fearless leader."

Kyle walked up to Jenny's desk, "Hello Jenny, I need to speak with the commissioner." Jenny had been so busy filing paperwork that she did not notice Kyle walk in, she laid down the paperwork she had been working on, and she pressed the intercom, "Detective Blake is here to see you, sir."

"Send him in Jenny."

Kyle entered the office and said, "When we arrived there were a few units in a hurry. Is something going on?"

Daniels looked at Kyle and replied, "No, actually there's a homeless guy out on the street begging for money, and he was causing a scene. Had quite a few complaints on him, so I sent a few units to make sure he does not cause any problems. Also, I did get your special forces team approved, the only issue is that they do not want you to wear any police uniforms, and they are getting you a building for your team."

With excitement Kyle answered, "Wow I am honored. I need to find Officer Hotz."

With a serious look on his face Commissioner Daniels said, "Officer Hotz mentioned that he suspected Mark Tritan kidnapped his son. It started a few years ago, I am sure you remember, Mark Tritan murdered two officers, he was a very smart scientist. He and his partner John Trueblood enjoyed experimenting on people. They were able to make a person not even look like a person, make them look like animals. Officer Hotz arrested Mark, we believe he kidnapped Carl to get revenge on James, he escaped from prison earlier this week, he created this experimental bioproduct that he named Exogenes. He created it a few years ago, before he was arrested. He created a deadly virus that he injected volunteers, his partner created a cure for the virus and that is when Mark killed John."

Kyle spoke up, "I guess with everything that has happened this year, that I forgot about that, I do remember it now. If you will excuse me, I need to go inform my team that we are up against an escaped convict who is out for revenge on Officer Hotz, I also need to meet up with Officer Hotz." Kyle left the office and went to find Maverick and Rhino, he was also looking around to see if Officer Hotz had arrived yet as well, "Okay guys, we are after an escaped convict who is trying to get revenge and kidnapped Carl Hotz, his name is Mark Tritan."

Suddenly two-gun shots were heard outside the police station, every Officer was running towards a crowd outside, Kyle sprinted towards the front entrance he thought, *"What else could happen? First a mad man and a monster kill a few people, and then I met a woman who I had become enamored with, and then I met a man who looks like a Rhinoceros, while I was at home a Starforce Officer appeared out of a portal. Come to find out the woman I became enamored with was a Starforce officer under cover, he called his Starforce team to help, we all joined forces with Starforce to take down the mad man; and earlier this week three criminals escape from prison and one of the convicts kidnap the son of a good friend and coworker, oh and let me not forget that a demon killed my partner and it seems like everyone had already forgotten about it, I am not sure how much weirder this can get."*

CHAPTER FOURTEEN

Kyle pushed his way through the large crowd of people and officers to get a glance at what the commotion had been about. Officer Johnson looked around at all the other officers standing by and in awe he said, "I think one of them is still alive."

Detective Stevens acknowledge, "Whatever it is, it doesn't look like a person, it looks like a porcupine, but the other is Officer Hotz."

Kyle finally pushed his way to the front of the crowd, but it had already been too late for Officer Hotz, he looked and saw Detective Stevens trying to get Officer Hotz breathing again by doing CPR on the lifeless body, but the gun shot penetrated his chest twice, Detective Stevens gave up and just sat next to Officer Hotz body, A loud boom caught everyone's attention- a sonic boom.

Officer Sanders pointed to the sky and everyone's attention focused to what he was pointing at, "Look, there's a falling star, which is strange; it is still daylight, and those are usually only able to be seen at night."

Kyle bent down to search for some identification on the porcupine's body, what he found belonged to Carl Hotz

The ambulances arrived and they loaded Officer Hotz in one ambulance and Carl Hotz in the other, and they drove them to the Colvidre hospital.

After the ambulances both drove away, Kyle remained there sitting on the curb, as he got up, he looked around and to his surprise, there was Maverick and Rhino standing right behind him.

Maverick spoke up, "I suspect we need to talk to that porcupine kid, because I think this is bigger than we originally thought."

Kyle nodded, "You are right, that porcupine kid is also Carl Hotz. The missing teenager we were assigned to look for, the man beside him was his father Officer Hotz, a good friend of mine. And after we talk to Carl, we will have to have a talk with Mark Tritan, if we can find him, let us go guys."

They got in Kyle's car and drove to the hospital.

Kyle went up to the information desk and asked the nurse, "We are here to see Carl Hotz an ambulance had just brought him in."

The nurse looked through the papers on her desk of all the new arrivals and replied, "He is being seen by the doctor now, but he is assigned to room 221. If you want to have a seat in the waiting room when he is wheeled to his room, his nurse will contact you."

Entering the elevator Kyle pressed the second-floor button, as the door closed it did not close smoothly, it moved slowly and clicked a few times. Maverick said, "I hope we make it to the second floor; this elevator looks like it is on its last leg."

The elevator stopped on the second floor with a jolt, and it squealed as the door reopened, Rhino glanced at Maverick, "That was a rough flight, I think I will take the stairs next time."

Looking in the room they noticed it was empty, they went and sat in the waiting room next to room 221. Rhino turned on the television, the volume for the television was not loud but easy to hear, the news lady on the channel said, "This is just in! A man with wings was spotted down at the northern bay area; we have a crew heading to the site right now; we will keep you posted when our crew arrives on site and gets the facts, stay tuned, the weather is next after these words from our sponsors."

Maverick replied, "A winged man huh? We need to go look into that."

Kyle answered, "Yes we do, but not now. We have to finish what we have come here for, and then we can check it out later, unless we are assigned to it before we are finished here."

A few minutes later a nurse walked in the room and said, "We are about to bring Mr. Hotz to his room, we will close the door and when we reopen the door, he will be ready for visitors."

Mark Tritan sitting behind a desk inside an old science laboratory named Axtek, when one of his loyal servants spoke up, "Master, Xtrobe is here to see you, like you had requested."

Tritan looked up from his desk and saw his loyal servant Rex, "Thank you."

Tritan stood up from his desk chair to meet with Xtrobe, "Thank you for coming as soon as you did. I am ready to collect the favor you owe me, I need you to kill Carl Hotz, he is in the Colvidre hospital room 221."

Peter Xtrobe a hired hit man, he somehow managed to connect a gun to his broken hand and now his right hand is a sniper gun, which is why he had been given the name assassin for hire, "After I kill Carl Hotz, I will no longer owe you any more favors and I will be able to go back to my own life, right?"

"That is correct after Carl Hotz is dead you will have completed all owed debts, and you will be a free assassin for hire."

The nurse walked in the waiting room and said, "Mr. Hotz is ready for visitors now."

Kyle entered the hospital room ad said, "Carl, I am Detective Kyle Blake, I was assisting your father in search for you, do you know what happened to your father?"

Carl began to tear up, "Yes, that evil man killed him."

Maverick replied, "Do you know the name of the evil man?"

Carl looked at Maverick and replied, "It was the same man who kidnapped me, he had great strength. We were inside a laboratory, but I can't remember where it is located at, but the room I was in will haunt me, it was bright white walls."

Kyle showed Carl some pictures he had of Mark Tritan, Carl replied, "That is the guy who killed my father, he kidnapped me and turned me into this monster, take me with you to find him. I want revenge on this evil man."

Kyle understood what it feels like to lose someone so close and want revenge, but he answered, "I don't think that is a promising idea, you need to stay here and get some rest. We will do our job and we will make him pay for his crimes that he's committed, he is an escaped criminal, also revenge is not as good as you think, it turns you against everyone and it doesn't make the pain go away, we need to leave you so you can rest."

As they were leaving the hospital Kyle said, "Now is a suitable time to look into that winged man by the northern bay area."

CHAPTER FIFTEEN

Arriving at northern bay area Maverick glanced around and said, "He is no longer here, we are too late."

They looked around for a little while and they did not find anything suspicious or anything to lead to where the winged man had gone to, Rhino looked towards the sky and replied, "The sun is setting and it will be getting dark fast, we need to get our rest. I have a feeling tomorrow is going to be a long day."

Kyle nodded, "You are right; let's go home, there is nothing more we can do here."

Peter Xtrobe walks in the Colvidre hospital looking down the hallways he notices cameras taking video of all movement in the hospital and he thought, *"There's no escaping for me, this is going to be a perplexing task."*

As he continued to walk down the halls, he finds the elevator and noticed behind him, there were nurses watching his every move. Looking down his right hand he knew the gun he connected to his hand is getting a lot of attention, *"Maybe connecting this gun to my hand was not a clever idea, good thing it is just clipped on my wrist."*

As he stepped out of the elevator and landed on the second floor, he overheard the nurse's radio, *"Keep an eye on the suspicious man when he exits the elevator, he has a gun."*

As he entered room 221, he noticed Carl Hotz was sleeping in the bed, as a hired mercenary he knows the risk, killing requires not to have a second thought. A nurse walks down the hallway and noticed Xtrobe at the entrance and yells, **"Security!"**

But it was already too late for the nurse Peter shot his gun at her hitting her in the stomach. A Security officer turned the corner and pointed his shinny pistol at Peter, "It's over, put down the gun and surrender or I will shoot you."

He began to count and before he could get to number two, Peter Xtrobe unclipped the gun and it slid off his wrist, revealing a wrist with no hand connected. The officer replied, "Get down on the floor and put your arms around your back, you are under arrest, anything you say can and will be used against you. If you cannot afford an attorney, one will be assigned to you. Do you understand?"

Peter has been arrested many times and knows the procedure very well, "Yes officer, I do."

One security officer removed Peter, as the nurse was put on a gurney and ran to see a doctor, due to the wound being a minor wound and not life threatening. The doctor ordered the nurse a room for a few days as they remove the bullet out of her stomach, the doctor told the nurse, "You will be fine in a couple of days." Carl Hotz slept through the assassination attempt on his life.

As the sun began to rise and lighten up the dark sky the Colvidre police department took on a unique look, the rock around the building glittered and sparkled, making the place take on a different look then when the sun sets, Kyle walks in the building followed by Maverick and Rhino, "Detective Kyle, the commissioner is waiting on you, he asked to speak with you when you had arrived this morning."

"Thank you, Officer Johnson. I am on my way there."

Commissioner Daniels motioned Kyle to enter his office, Kyle said, "Commissioner, these are my partners, Maverick and Rhino."

To show his personable personality he stood up and extended his right hand to shake their hands, "It is nice to meet you two, and I wanted to see you to let you know I am assigning someone else to be your partner as well."

Surprised Kyle answered, "Who is it?" Daniels folded his hands as he sat back down at his desk, "It is Carl Hotz, someone tried to kill him last night, we currently have a few officers on guard. Keeping him safe."

Curious Maverick replied, "Do you know who tried to kill him?"

"Yes, we do, his name is Peter Xtrobe he was an inmate with Mark Tritan, and they escaped prison together a few days ago with Matthew Fusion, he is not talking at the moment."

Not surprised Kyle answered, "Is Investigator Jackson trying to get him to talk?"

Daniels cracked a smile, "Of course he is the best at it." Jenny interrupted, "Excuse me, we just had another sighting of the winged man, he was spotted by the old sound traxx warehouse."

"Kyle, you heard it, find out what this is about. I will continue to have my officers keep Carl safe until he is released to your team, he may be a key to some of this madness." As Kyle left the office he said, "Thank you Commissioner."

As they walked to the main hallway they passed Detective Watkins, Kyle asked, "Can you get me the file on John Trueblood?"

Detective Watkins answered, "Is that one of the guys that Mark Tritan killed?" Kyle added, "Yes he was also his partner, I have to get going, when you get the file, could you put it on your desk, and I will retrieve it later."

CHAPTER SIXTEEN

Mark Tritan a scientist who has started experimenting on people, he once experimented on animals but has decided to mix the two together, most of the people he experiments on if they survive, are made to where he could control them. And if he loses that power over them, he either kills them or wipes their memory, Mark Tritan calls his laboratory Axtek.

Mark Tritan is standing close by the feet of a body he has strapped in on one of his experimental tables, not much is known about the guy, he is unable to speak. Tritan has given him the name Chaos, he wears a mask Tritan has removed his mask and underneath the mask he is a blue skinned alien, Tritan has been trying to force him to speak but he has no mouth, Tritan said, "I am going to experiment on you and make you a voice box, that will give you the ability to speak. Not that you have a choice."

Secretly Chaos wanted to be able to speak he has no memory of why he is on Colvidre. Tritan's loyal servant Rex says, "Master,

Xtrobe got himself arrested and didn't finish his job."

Tritan was disappointed in Xtrobe and replied, "Rex, I need you to go finish the job, kill Xtrobe and Carl Hotz." Bowing his head he answered, "Yes Master."

As they arrived at the old Sound Traxx building Maverick glanced around and said, "This building looks abandoned."

Kyle answered, "Let's get out and look around, see if there are any clues to where the winged man is going next, or maybe he is here hiding."

As Kyle looked around inside the building he found a piece of newspaper on the floor, the name Axtek was highlighted with the address underneath the name 12538 West Sigma Street, "There is no sign of the winged man in here, but I did find a clue."

Rhino replied, "There are only four houses around and they are all empty, this is like a deserted area, I haven't seen life anywhere."

Kyle said, "I found an address highlighted on this newspaper, let's go check it out guys."

Maverick replied, "Maybe, we should go to the hospital and check on Carl Hotz, Like the commissioner said he might be a clue to all this." Kyle agreed.

As Rex walked the same halls in the hospital as Xtrobe, Rex is short and the way he walks makes him look as though he had a hunchback, he has a scarred face short black hair and brown eyes, he would be a frightening site if found in a dark alley, as he stopped at Carl's room, he noticed a few officers sitting in the waiting room next to Carl's room, and he thought, *"This is not going to be easy, officers could kill me after I kill Carl, but here it goes."*

As he enters the room, he notices Carl laying on the bed, Officer Sanders stood up and replied, "Can I help you?" Rex blurted out a laugh and said, "No, I am beyond help." Pulling out his gun he shot Officer Sanders in the leg, forcing him to fall to the ground and he takes aim for Carl.

Officer Young turns the corner and shots Rex in the left shoulder forcing him to drop the gun while in extreme pain. Officer Young put his handcuffs on Rex, not caring about the pain he was in due to the shoulder shot.

Even being the son of a police officer Carl was not use to gun fire so close, it had frightened him, Kyle heard the commotion as he was getting out of the elevator and they all three hurried to Carl's room, Officer Young explained to him what all took place, as Officer Sanders was taken to his own hospital room. The other officers that had been sitting in the waiting room took Rex away.

Officer Young asked, "Kyle are you going to be here for a little bit?" He nodded and Officer Young continued, "Then I am going to give Commissioner Daniels an update."

Kyle sat next to Carl and said, "Are you ready to get out of here? I can arrange it." Carl smiled and replied, "Yes please, I want to get out of here before I die." Kyle got up and motioned for Carl to get up, "Then let's leave the room, so he can get dressed."

Rhino tossed his stuff to him and said, "Welcome to the team kid."

Kyle said, "When we leave here, I need to go back to the police department real fast, to read a file I requested." Kyle was referring to the file on John Trueblood that he asked Detective Watkins to pull for him.

Hearing the news about Rex, Tritan became incredibly angry, "I told him no loose ends, he is too weak. He will tell the police everything he knows, he must die as well now, my best bet is to send Deadshot." He is another assassin for hire, he rarely gets caught, he is the best but the most expensive to hire.

Seraph the winged man is on top of the Axtek building, he has been searching for a way inside, finding a window on the roof had been the only entrance he found, and it led to a room, which had looked like it used to be an office, he quietly broke the window enough so he could crawl through. As he looked around the room, he noticed it had not been used for some time, opening the top drawer on the desk and found a business card it read, Axtek Science Laboratory John Trueblood and Mark Tritan 557-8394 Research and experimental drugs 25 years of experience.

Seraph thought, *"It's now or never, I know I am here on a mission, but this guy has got to be stopped before it is too late."* Since the door has not been opened in a long time as Seraph opened the door it creaked, Tritan turned around and saw Seraph standing at the office door he said, "I heard about you on the news, what do you want?"

Seraph puffed his chest and replied, "Tritan I am Seraph, I was sent here to Colvidre on a mission, but I decided to find you and stop you from doing all the evil you do in the future."

Tritan acted dumb founded, "I don't do evil, I just give people what they want, and that is power." Seraph laughed, "You killed your partner John Trueblood, and all these people you experiment on, you will pay for this, your sins will be your own undoing."

Tritan jolted towards Seraph, and as his punch got close Seraph flew out of the way dodging the punch. They engage in a battle between good and evil, Seraph flew downward towards Tritan hitting him in the cheek.

Detective Watkins saw Kyle and said, "I pulled the file you requested." Handing him the file he added, "When you are finished with it, you can just lay it on my desk, and I will return it to the file room." Kyle nodded and replied, "Good thing not every file got burnt, we would be in trouble. Have you heard anything about Commander Jurgon?"

Detective Watkins answered, "No, it is tragic, what he did was wrong. I think that they might offer him a second chance."

"I hope they do; I think there is a good officer inside him." Kyle felt no hard feelings for Commander Jurgon, he opened the file and started reading. File: John Trueblood Axtek scientist 8 years ago, he helped the police arrest Mark Tritan, his fellow scientist and partner, when Mark Tritan served his time, he was released from prison, and he killed John Trueblood. A government agent who worked for an organization called L.E.A. took the body of John Trueblood.

There was nothing else in the file, Maverick pointed at the newspaper that they picked up when they were investigating the old sound traxx building, "Here is the address for the Axtek Science Laboratory it is highlighted."

Kyle said, "Axtek that building is still around, we will go look inside the laboratory. Maverick put your armor on, we are going to need all the help we can get." Rhino answered, "Maybe we will also discover the secret about the winged man, that we have been hearing about."

Tritan hit Seraph in the gut, a blow that caused Seraph to grab a hold of his stomach, Tritan kicked him in the left leg, right above the knee cap. Seraph curled his fingers into a fist and he threw an upper cut shot at Tritan, hitting him in the jaw. Tritan lost his breath for a moment, and when he caught it again, he said, "You caught me off guard, it will not happen again." Tritan laughed and motioned for someone, and from the shadows came a snake like creature, Tritan calls him Reaver. He was a crimson guard for Tritan, he had mutated him to look like a snake. As he came out of the shadows, he hit Seraph with a metal beam, and it knocked Seraph unconscious.

Suddenly the door flew open and standing at the door was a man named Hightower, he looks like a business type guy wearing a business suit and tie. He stood about five foot nine inches tall, short light brown hair, a blonde color and well groomed.

Tritan looked at Hightower and laughed, Seraph had awakened, and Tritan said, "Is this your backup or is this your lawyer? You will need one when I am through with you."

Hightower interrupted him, "Are you done with your jokes?" Tritan looked back at Seraph who had been tied up to the wall thanks to Reaver, and then he looked back at Hightower and replied, "I guess." Hightower said, "Let my buddy there go or else." Tritan shifted his eyes to Seraph and answered, "I can't let him go, so I guess that leaves the or else option." Hightower nodded, "I expected you would say that. Everyone that knows me calls me Hightower, and it is time you find out why."

Before he finished speaking, he started growing fast, when he had finally stopped growing, he was standing twelve feet tall, "I can grow taller than this, but this size will do just fine." Hightower punched Tritan in the gut, the hit was so hard that it sent Tritan flying, hitting the wall behind, he was down for the count.

Hightower took this time to go release the prisoners, he first went to Seraph and after he had released him, he looked at the experimenting table and saw another body laying on the table, and the guy had wires and hoses connected to his body, Hightower felt sorry for him and set him free also.

Reaver slithered out of the dark corner and ran towards Seraph, he kicked Reaver on the right side of his rib cage, knocking him to the ground, he slithered away as fast as he could, like only a snake can do.

Tritan came to his senses and stood up and grabbed a syringe, he started to sneak up to Hightower and got ready to stick the syringe in his leg, when suddenly Kyle, Maverick, Rhino and Carl stepped into the laboratory.

Kyle pointed his gun at Tritan and said, "Freeze Tritan, you are under arrest." Tritan dropped the syringe, and Tritan revealed that he had a pistol as he pulled it out and aimed it, Kyle then added, "Tritan, drop the gun or I will shoot."

Chaos regained conscious and got up from the table and looked around, his stare put fear in the hearts of everyone in the room, it was as if he was able to investigate everyone's soul, he glanced at Kyle and Tritan and without a word they both dropped their guns, like he told them to drop them without saying a word.

Tritan and Kyle just stood there like they were in a trance, Rhino took this time to duck down and charge at Tritan, the impact knocked Tritan back and he landed on the floor, Carl shot a few quills out of his body, as those quills hit Tritan, they made him weaker, he was unable to stand very well, stumbling to stand up he said, "This is far from over." After he had finished saying that he disappeared through a portal. Chaos wandered off by himself disappearing in the evening.

Seraph put his hand out to shake Kyle's hand, "Kyle I am Seraph, and I was sent here on a mission, and this is Hightower, I met him here on Colvidre."

Carl looked around and said, "Now that I had revenge on the man who did this to me and killed my father, I feel lost I don't know what to do now." Kyle nodded, "Revenge can kill a person, but sometimes after you get revenge and close a chapter, you feel dead inside, Revenge should never take precedence in one's life, Seraph, you and Hightower are welcome to join my team."

Seraph entertained that thought for a split second, but replied, "I can't, my mission is my own responsibility, and it has just started, you will see me again, my friend." Seraph and Hightower left the building together. Carl looked down to the ground and said, "Now that I do not have to worry about Tritan hiring someone to kill me, I am going to leave your team and live with my mother for a while. I think she will need me to help her through the death of my father and her husband, we both need to be able to comfort each other through this challenging time, I will see you later."

Watching Carl leave Kyle said, "I am ready for a vacation already, things have been getting strange lately, Maverick, you and Rhino have rooms at the Sunset hotel and spa, all that you guys require will be paid for, just go to the front desk and tell them your names and they have the rooms assigned to you, compliments of the Colvidre police department."

Maverick replied, "I think it is time to call it a day, we have all had a long day." Rhino grabbed a hold of Maverick as they flew to the hotel. The evening sky began to turn orange as the sun was setting and all the streetlights lit up the night sky and the reflections of the streetlights in the windows of all the buildings made the city

of Colvidre well lit. As the police arrived
Kyle replied, "There is nothing left for me to
do here, I am going home also."

Officer Young found Kyle before he left and
said, "Kyle, I thought you would want to
know that the guys who tried to assassinate
Carl Hotz in the hospital are gone.
Somehow, they disappeared."

CHAPTER SEVENTEEN

It is very dark for this time of year as a new morning has started, even with the glare of the streetlights reflecting through the windows, Commander Firestar came out of a portal, and he noticed no one had been around and the dark sky hid his entrance. Pressing his star communicator he replied, "It is clear, send my team." Starforce answered, "Understood." Another portal opened on the left side of Firestar and two Starforce officers came out of the portal, both were loaded with weapons. Crystal and Firearm he can turn his whole body into flames at his will. Firestar nodded, "Okay team Prince Derek has sent us to find Maverick, Dark Avenger has returned, and we need the help of Maverick and his new friends, we need all the help we can get, he will not be as easy to capture this time around, since Vanisher has teamed up with him." Firearm looked at Firestar and said, "So where do we start?" Crystal replied, "Kyle works for the local law enforcers here on Colvidre, we will begin to look for him there." Firestar nodded in agreement.

There was a knock on the door to the Special Forces office, sitting behind the desk is Kyle and he replied, "Hey Rhino, could you get the door." Rhino opened the door and standing at the door was Seraph and Hightower, as they walked inside the office Seraph said, "We are going to need your team's assistance."

Kyle stood up and said, "You are welcome to the team, we are honored to have you two join the team." Maverick said puzzled, "What kind of mission are you on that you need our help?" Seraph answered, "I was sent here to save Colvidre, a demon from my world will come and try to take over this world, and I have come to stop him."

Rhino chuckled, "Yeah, that seems like every bad guy's dream, just to take over the world." Kyle question, "A demon? A demon had killed my partner, but that had been a few months ago, and nothing was ever heard of the demon again." Seraph replied, "I am truly sorry Kyle, I didn't know he had already been on Colvidre."

On a side street in Colvidre a portal opened and a man from Dalmir came out of the portal, he has a diamond shape on his chest, he has a blue tooth talking device connected to his ear. He was a Starforce officer at one time, his name is Drifter. He is a scout for the Dark Avenger, he came to Colvidre with Firestar to get Maverick to help Starforce with a bad guy, when King Melach's brother tried to kill him. That is when Maverick created Starforce's computers and most of their weapons, he is here this time to find a few bad guys to help and join his team. He was sent to find Carl Hotz and Chaos, Drifter spoke into his Bluetooth, "Viper, tell the Dark Avenger that I made it safe, I don't think Starforce has figured out what happened yet, so they have no clue that I am here, unless they detected my portal, if they do find out that I am here on Colvidre, I will need some help, my teleporter has malfunctioned, or something is interfering with the signal." Viper answered, "I will look into it on this side, and see if the problem is on this side. I will see if I can send you some assistance to help you teleport the new recruits when you find them."

Firestar told his team, "Let's separate, I will go inside the Colvidre police department, and find Maverick, you guys blend in with the crowd and keep watch, look normal until I return." Leaving his team outside the building, he walked inside to the front desk and said, "Excuse me." The lady behind the desk looked up and Firestar continued, "Do you know where I can find Kyle Blake or Maverick?" The lady answered, "Yes sir, they are both on the second floor, inside the special forces office room 201." Firestar nodded, "Thank you." He walked to the elevator pressing the call button and waiting on the elevator door to open so he could take it to the second floor.

In a hurry a man named Venus is jogging through the Starforce building, he has the same rank as Firestar, only he does not have a team yet, he had led some officers as needed. The familiar hallways are just a blur as he searches for Prince Derek, he has some serious news that he has to deliver to the Prince, he just left the royal chambers since it was empty, he had first searched the archery stalls outside the building, there is only one more room the Prince could be in and it is the Throne room, Venus entered the Throne room and caught a glimpse of Prince Derek, he took a knee to bow before the Prince, he remained on his knees to catch his breath, he had searched everywhere, and the Throne room was the last place to look since he is rarely inside he is normally practicing archery at the range behind the castle, "Prince, I have news I was scanning the sector when the computers detected a portal open on Colvidre. As I investigated the portal a little closer and did some cross referencing, I noticed that it was Drifter who came out of the portal. Dark Avenger sent him to Colvidre to look for Carl Hotz, one of Kyle Blake's team members who helped capture the Dark Avenger when he was after Crystal looking for the lost heir of planet Mist, there are a few more people he is searching for, but I do not recognize them. I still have been unsuccessful in locating Vanisher since he had left Planet Valtone. I have a theory that he had joined forces with the Dark Avenger, but we also thought that was the case when the Dark Avenger went to find Crystal, and he was actually still on Valtone." Prince Derek nodded, "Yeah, we did jump to conclusions a little too soon last time. We need to send a small team to assist Firestar on Colvidre, we need to inform Firestar what we suspect their plans are and who they are searching for, and hopefully we can get to them first. Venus, I am sending a three-man team to Colvidre to assist Firestar and his team, I want you to take Xamot and Colonel Savage, and you will lead the team. Good luck you are going to need it, I will inform the King about this at once." Venus lowered his head as he left to get Xamot, and Colonel Savage as requested by Prince Derek.

"Guys, I need to meet up with Commissioner Daniels and check in with him, I will return shortly." As he left the Special forces office he looked around and noticed how many things have changed within the last few months. Maverick asked Hightower, "How tall can you actually grow?" Hightower looked around and replied, "I have grown as tall as the Empire Galactic building." Maverick knows that building better than anyone knows he use to work in that building before joining Starforce, all kinds of government officials gather in that building, it is the tallest building on Colvidre.

The door to the office opened and standing at the door was Firestar. Surprised Maverick said, "Firestar what are you doing here?" Firestar answered, "Hello Maverick, my team and I have come to get the aide of your team, the Dark Avenger has escaped, we haven't figured out how he escaped yet, but we are looking into it. Prince Derek thought it would be a clever idea to gather the aide of this team to help capture him again." Rhino replied, "The Dark Avenger again?" Firestar nodded. Kyle walked back in the office, "Okay guys, there's a report about a suspicious looking man, he was seen on North Majahony Avenue, we are going to check it out." Kyle felt eyes on him, and he turned around and noticed Firestar, "Firestar, what are you doing here?"

He answered, "Dark Avenger escaped, and we need your team to assist us." Kyle replied, "We have to check out the report of a suspicious man, if you want to join us, and then after we finish, we will be able to help you." Firestar agreed, "I will get my team, and we will meet you on North Majahony Avenue."

CHAPTER
EIGHTEEN

Venus had finished getting him team together, Xamot can run fast, a lot like Firestar. Colonel Savage is super strong, but he is not the smartest. Prince Derek motioned for Venus and his team to gather around him, "You guys know your mission; the King has approved it, go to Colvidre and assist Firestar." Venus and his team disappeared through a portal.

Drifter had found Carl Hotz and he stopped him and said, "Carl, I am Drifter, my leader had sent me to find you here on Colvidre, will you join my team?"

Carl just got used to living with his mother since his father was killed, he said, "Um, I don't know." After he had finished speaking Kyle and his team showed up, "Freeze, you are under arrest. Back away from Carl Hotz."

Venus and his small team appeared out of a portal in the middle of all the commotion, so much had happened that Carl got confused and frightened, he is not in control of his abilities and out of fear he shot four quills out of his body, one of the quills hit Xamot, the other three hit Colonel Savage, the quill needles inject poison when they stick into something, they do not come out very easy, the design of quills are to enter and exit different areas, they rarely come out the same way they go in. Xamot fell to the ground in pain, Venus looked at Colonel Savage and he was not moving, running up to Colonel Savage he bent down to check on him, Drifter pointed at Carl and said, "We have to go now." He grabbed Carl and disappeared.

A frustrated Firestar said, "Venus, what are you doing here?" He answered, "Prince Derek sent me here to warn you, that Drifter is here looking for Carl Hotz and some guy named Chaos, my team was sent here to assist you, now if you will excuse me, I need to attend to my team." Firestar glanced at Xamot and Colonel Savage knowing they needed medical attention he pressed his communicator, "Starforce, teleport Xamot and Colonel Savage, they are in need of medical attention." The two disappeared.

There are personal security guards for King Melach and Prince Derek, they are called Sentry guards, it is a separate division of Starforce, their only mission is to protect royalty. One of Prince Derek's sentry guards said, "Your highness, Xamot and Colonel Savage both were injured during their mission." Prince Derek replied, "Guardian, come with me, we are going to Colvidre to help Firestar and Venus." With a turn of his head, he noticed Vortex, a Starforce officer standing next to him, "Vortex get a portal ready; Guardian and I are both going to Colvidre to assist Venus and Firestar."

Vortex nodded, he had been tainted he used to be sincere as a Starforce Officer, Prince Derek had not known that he had been the spy for Dark Avenger, his parents were killed, he was told that Starforce killed them, but he was already an Officer and the Dark Avenger convinced him to remain as an Officer, but to leak information to the Dark Avenger, he is the reason that Dark Avenger knew where to find Crystal and that she may have known where to find the lost heir to the planet Mist.

Dark Avengers space craft is still buried in the sewers under the streets on Colvidre, Dark Avenger has been hiding in his space craft for some time now, he looked at

Vanisher, "You also went into hiding after Starforce defeated you and King Chalem, now is our time to take over Starforce, Vortex just informed me that Prince Derek is taking Guardian with him to come here to Colvidre, that puts most of Starforce's powerful Officers out of the Starforce Castle, we will start by destroying Starforce's computers and communications, they will be stuck on Colvidre."

Vanisher said, "What about Northstar?" A laugh bellowed out of Dark Avenger as he said, "He is of no concern to me, once we have King Melach captured Northstar will not be difficult."

King Melach motioned for Dexter he said, "My son is going to Colvidre, I want you to go with him and keep me informed on everything that is going on there. I was sent to Colvidre when I was around his age to find my wife. I know how bad that place can become." He was reminded of the time he was sent to Colvidre to find his wife, his father wanted him to find a perfect wife to help rule, and he found Elizabeth, it had been a shame when his own brother killed her to try and take over the kingdom, Anger swelled up inside King Melach just thinking of what they went through together as a family.

Drifter looked around the abandoned building he called his hideout and said to Carl, "I still have another recruit to locate, and then my first task is over, if you are going to be a part of my team then I will call you." He thought for a moment and added, "Quill, since that is what your needles are called." Quill smiled and nodded his head in agreement and approval of the name. Vanisher appeared and looked around, "I expected you to have found both recruits by now, we must go find this Chaos."

Kyle said, "Firestar, what is going on here?" Firestar replied, "We must join forces again to capture the Dark Avenger again and this time he has help, a guy named Vanisher, also Drifter is aiding them as well. They are creating an army for some reason."

Prince Derek, Guardian, and Dexter appeared out of a portal, Guardian is tall and muscular, he has super strength. Firestar looked at Prince Derek and replied, "Prince Derek, what are you doing here?" He knew he did not have time to answer all the questions that he would face, "Colvidre, is not the target, Vanisher has joined forces with the Dark Avenger and Drifter, they are searching for an alien called Chaos." Firestar added, "I know Prince, but it is not safe here for you." Guardian spoke up, "I am here to protect Prince Derek and make sure no harm will come to him."

Firestar nodded in approval knowing that Guardian was one of Prince Derek's personal Sentry guards and that he would lay his life down to protect the prince at all costs, he said, "Thank you for coming Guardian. Prince Derek doesn't understand how dangerous this place can be."

King Melach heard whispers recently of an army capturing all the Starforce officers, it was happening all so fast. His Sentry guards were the only officers left, he said,

"Commander Hawk?" looking around he noticed he had no sentry guards to protect him. The Dark Avenger appeared outside of the throne room and said, "Your Majesty, I have taken over the castle, all your beloved starforce officers are already in the prison cells, along with your sentry guards, you are all that is left of the old way. Surrender and I will not let anything happen to you, you will live to see the fall of this kingdom, and I will have my revenge for the assassination of my father."

King Melach surrendered and said, "Who's your father?" The Dark Avenger added, "Mevila, the loyal advisor to King Savante, who was assassinated by Northstar."

King Melach had just realized that everything that has been happening all revolves around the lost heir to the planet Mist.

One of Dark Avengers loyal subjects his name is Crimson Guard he forced King Melach into a prison cell, King Melach noticed most of the prison cells are full of Officers, he noticed not all officers are here, some most have either died in battle or in hiding.

Vortex was wiping the Starforce communications so no communication will be allowed for any Starforce officer, already on a mission or trying to communicate to the castle. As he moved to the Starforce computers and records he backed up all information to a small disk drive before he wiped the information from the hard drive, he saw some information it was revealed Dark Avengers real name is Aligon Spartan and it said he was arrested for the murder of Vortex's parents, it said he believed they had information to find the last heir of planet Mist, it came of a shock to him, he was told that his parents were murdered by Starforce, it also said he had a brother named Drifter. After the disk saved Starforce's information, he grabbed it and put it in his pocket and disappeared through a portal.

Unaware of Vortex's actions, Dark Avenger sent a message to Starforce on Colvidre, "I have taken over Starforce headquarters, there is no way to return to save Starforce, I have a king to kill and Prince Derek if you know what is good for you, you will remain there and not try to come back."

Hearing the message Prince Derek got upset, "I should have been there and not here. I played right into the Dark Avenger's plan." Firestar pat his back to comfort him, "The King wouldn't want you there, and if our King dies, he will want you here so we can return to Dalmir and take his place as the King of Dalmir and leader of Starforce, we need to come up with a plan to take back our rightful place." Guardian said, "Dark Avenger took over Starforce and we are stuck here, since we are unable to open any portals, how are we going to help?" Crystal answered, "My son Northstar is still on Dalmir, he will find a way to save our King."

Finding Chaos Drifter said, "Chaos, I have been searching for you to ask you to join our evil team." Chaos could not speak, he is an alien without a mouth, wearing a mask to hide his face. Quill looked at Drifter and said, "You're a bad guy? I don't belong here; I am a good guy." Vanisher impatiently said,

"Enough I will banish you; to another dimension to give you time to think about your decisions." He knocked Chaos in the head, a blow that threw him against the building behind him. Immediately a portal opened, and Vortex appeared he said, "Vanisher, I banish you from Colvidre." As he opened a portal below Vanisher fierce winds came out and sucked him through it closed as he disappeared. "Drifter, I have discovered some information about both of us, it says that you are my brother and that our parents were murdered by the Dark Avenger seeking information from them."

Drifter answered, "I suspected we were brothers but had no evidence to confirm it." Vortex said, "Dark Avenger has taken over Starforce, I have betrayed Starforce, I helped him take over the castle, we need to help rescue King Melach and restore Starforce back to the way it was." Drifter nodded as he looked around and noticed Chaos had disappeared, "Quill, come with us help us save Starforce."

King Melach began pacing back and forth in the prison cell and he said, "I am not only a

King, but I also went through Starforce training when I was younger, I will never forget all the things that I learned, and all the fighting moves. Let us escape, who is with me?"

Looking around the cell revealed the three officers who were in the same cell, Commander Hawk, Northstar, and Storm Shadow.

Storm Shadow was an experiment gone perfectly wrong, he was originally created for evil, he had been cloned by some of the perfect warriors known on Colvidre, but he escaped to Dalmir where he joined Starforce in hopes to return to Colvidre and find the government project known as L.E.A. and destroy the program.

Commander Hawk is a commanding Officer for King Melach's personal sentry guards, sworn to protect the King at all costs. Northstar a great Starforce officer and the son of Crystal.

Commander Hawk said, "Your Majesty, I have sworn an oath to protect you at all costs, you know we will not stay here and let you risk your life for ours." Storm Shadow nodded. Northstar stood up, "We must take back Starforce and capture the Dark Avenger before things get worse than they have already."

Storm Shadow looked around the cell in hopes of finding a way out, it was an underground cell, no windows or sunlight, the only way out in through the entrance. King Melach said, "I know every leak and mouse hole in these cells, there is a huge drainpipe right below your feet Commander Hawk."

Commander Hawk figured that was the way out, so he pulled out a silent pocket bomb the size of a dime, that was originally created by Maverick, he laid the bomb on the ground right above where the drainpipe was located per King Melach, he set it to go off in about five seconds to give them enough time to move to safety. Suddenly the cell under the bomb began to crumble revealing the drainpipe spoken by King Melach. Commander Hawk jumped down the drain first to make sure it was safe for the King to enter, he nodded and the rest of Starforce in the cell followed, flipping on his flashlight they started their escape.

Suddenly as they started seeing sunlight at the end of the drainpipe, a portal opened and Vortex, Drifter and Quill appeared from the portal, Drifter said, "Your Majesty, we mean you no harm, I apologize for betraying you and Starforce." Vortex added, "We have come to take you to Colvidre and reunite you with Prince Derek, so we can come up with a plan to take over our home."

King Melach nodded and thought, *"They are serious I have never heard these two guys call this place home."* As Vortex opened a portal to Colvidre, they all disappeared.

CHAPTER NINETEEN

Near the Colvidre Police department a portal opens, and they appeared from Dalmir, King Melach said, "Drifter, why did you save my life?" Drifter knew he would have to answer this question at least one more time and so he replied, "Vortex discovered information that said the Dark Avenger had killed our parents, we had always been told Starforce killed them, it also said that Vortex and I are brothers, I was never told that I had a brother." King Melach remembered when that occurred, "I kind of remember that it happened when Dark Avenger first betrayed Starforce, he began his quest to locate the lost heir of Mist, Starforce tried to hide you two, but the Dark Avenger found you anyway." Northstar said, "We need to go find Prince Derek and the rest of Starforce." Commander Hawk agreed, "Let's go."

Crimson Guard a loyal servant of the Dark Avenger was shaking in his bright red clothing, as he entered the throne room; he could change his body to blend in with the background, a lot like a chameleon, he was the bearer of shocking news he hopes his loyalty is remembered after he gives the shocking news, "Sir." He bowed before the Dark Avenger still trembling, he continued, "King Melach escaped, and Northstar is with him."

The Dark Avenger began to become terribly angry, but he managed to calm down enough to look like he was not angry and replied, "Who let him escape and how did he escape?" The tension between Crimson Guard and the Dark Avenger had lifted and he answered, "Boss, there is a hole in the bottom of the cell, which revealed a large tunnel below." As he made a fist you could hear the bones of Crimson Guard crack and when he closed his fist the body exploded into tiny pieces, "If anyone else fails me or decides to bring me any more unwelcome news, I will destroy them like I did my loyal servant. Where is Vortex? And why hasn't Vanisher checked in with me?"

On a planet named Kora a portal opened, and Vanisher appeared being thrown out of the portal by a gust of wind. He thought to himself, *"Why can't I open a portal, I am unable to teleport out of here, something is wrong. What planet am I on?"* The planet or the aliens on the planet have caused him not to be able to use his teleporting ability. Suddenly, thousands of little red alien creatures came out of the tall grass they spoke in an alien language, "Gluf ot un op kegad." The translation "Grab him and take him to our King." All the little aliens grabbed Vanisher who was still trying to gather his sight, the vertigo he was feeling had put him in a weakened state, they carried him to their palace.

Seraph looking out the window of the Colvidre police department said, "Out of the shadows the evil one will return, he will try to destroy everything we have created, Hellfire the prince of darkness, an alien like no other, and we are not ready for such a creature." Prince Derek replied, "I can't stand waiting any longer, we need to find a way back to Dalmir." He was pacing back and forth in the office, the door opened wide and standing at the entrance is King

Melach, Prince Derek looked up and said, "Father! You are alive and here on Colvidre." Tears welled up in his eye blurring his vision, it was a heavy burden being lifted from his chest, he knew he was not ready to be King of Dalmir, realizing now that it is time to step up and be the prince he was raised to be, as he is waiting to take over the throne. King Melach answered, "Yes, thanks to Drifter and Vortex."

Firestar said, "Drifter, I am sorry for kicking you off the force, I had thought you turned against us, and started feeding information to the Dark Avenger." Vortex replied, "We both revealed vital information to the Dark Avenger, I was the one who told him that Crystal was on Colvidre looking for the lost heir, we were told that Starforce had killed our parents until we found evidence to support otherwise."

Northstar saw Crystal and said, "Mother, be careful, I don't want to lose you again." Crystal kissed her son's cheek and replied, "I have been careful, and I don't plan on changing a thing." Venus interrupted saying, "Vortex, you have the ability to open portals, right?" He exclaimed, "Yes, we can return home, and take the fight to our home." He added, "Dark Avenger had me delete all the files, but I backed up all the files on this disk drive, so we can upload the files back onto the computers, he has no clue that I have all your files saved."

King Melach said, "Thank you again Vortex. We will have Maverick boot up our computers and get them up and going again." Commander Hawk questioned Vortex, "You're not coming with us? We could use your ability to defeat the Dark Avenger." Answering he said, "I am coming with you guys, I helped make this mess, but when he finds out I betrayed him, he will kill me." Commander Hawk replied, "We are a team, we will protect you like a brother." He stopped for a moment and turned to Drifter, "What about you?"

Drifter said, "I am considering joining the Diamond Enforcers on Wildwood, I want you guys to meet Quill, I found him here on Colvidre." Kyle said, "Quill I like the name, it has a ring to it. The offer to join my team is still there for you." He replied, "Kyle, this adventure has awakened me, and I realize that I would be honored to be a part of your team." King Melach said, "Let's go take our home world back, we will have freedom once again after we defeat the Dark Avenger."

Dark Avenger began getting impatient and started pacing back and forth he said, "Kahl, find Vortex for me, I want him to go to Colvidre and find Starforce. I want them all dead except for King Melach and Prince Derek, I want to gather all the information that they have on the lost heir before I kill them personally, has anyone seen Vanisher since he went to help Drifter, oh that is right I have not seen Drifter either. Blaze, I need you to see if you can locate Drifter and Vanisher." Blaze answered, "Yes sir." Gracefully she floated out of the room, he found her on a planet hiding from her family and friends since they wanted to kill her, they decided she was a witch and needed purged from existence."

Vortex opened a portal and said, "Okay guys, let's go." As they disappeared and the portal closed, a shadowed figure walked out of the shadows, after he had watched everyone leave and said, "It has begun, and I will create havoc on Colvidre, while all the heroes are no longer on Colvidre." The mysterious person disappeared as quickly as he appeared.

The portal opened in the training room where the student's study to become Starforce officers, Firestar looked around and said, "I am so glad this place is in one piece; I had thought, he would have burnt it down by now." Vortex said, "I had hoped this room was empty, since it would be a good place to produce a plan of attack. Dark Avenger does not know that you are here, I am going to go check in, and maybe we can attack him while he is unprepared, also I will distract him and try to get some of our weapons back." Venus blurted, "Get the freeze ray, it came in handy against him the last time."

Inside the Dark Avengers space craft, Blaze is frantically looking for Drifter's presence on Colvidre, she turned on the communicator and said, "Sir, I can't find Drifter anywhere, I am currently inside your space craft." Dark Avenger started to be irritated that she went all the way to his space craft, and he said, "You and Psyblade come back, I need you two here with me and the rest of my team."

Viper spotted Vortex walking in the hallway, "The master is looking for you." Vortex nodded, "I know, I have some news for the master, but first I need to go to the weapons room, tell him I will meet him in the communications room in 10 minutes." Viper agreed.

Viper entered the throne room and said, "Master, I have found Vortex, he said he has some news for you, and to meet him in the communications room." He grinned with approval, knowing that Viper had been loyal to him.

Vortex opened a portal in the weapons room, and Starforce appeared, as they were grabbing weapons Vortex said, "I have a plan. I will open a portal right outside the communications room, where the Dark

Avenger will be waiting for me, I will have his attention and will buy you guys time to go inside and fire the freeze ray at Viper and anyone else you can, Storm Shadow you shoot a ultra-violent ray and heat up the door to prevent anyone from distracting us, where we can capture the Dark Avenger once again." Firestar added, "Sounds like a good plan, let's go."

He opened a portal as he said he would right outside the communications room, Vortex walked up to the Dark Avenger and he said, "I followed King Melach and he escaped to Colvidre, I came back as soon as I could to give you this information."

Dark Avenger replied, "Well we will have to gather our forces and kill them on Colvidre." Immediately after he said that Commander Hawk walked in the room, he fired the freeze ray at Viper turning him into a block of ice, Storm Shadow then fired the ultra-violent ray that Maverick had created for Starforce on the door. It became so hot that it would burn anyone who got closer than six feet to the door. Dark

Avenger laughed and clapped his hands, "Impressive, you caught me off guard, Vortex I am disappointed in you and Drifter, but I knew this time would come, that you two would betray me." As he finished speaking, he shot a blast of energy from the palm of his right hand at Vortex, hitting him and knocking him to the ground with such a force that the walls around the room shook. Maverick took this opportunity to hit him with all his might, making the Dark Avenger hit the ground also, that is when Firestar shot the freeze ray at him freezing him solid. Vortex got up and shook himself off, "That was a powerful shot." Vortex opened a portal to planet Ethien, there are no signs of intelligent life on this planet, a planet under the watch of Starforce, it is close to the deep core regions of space. The planets full of green blobs and no telling what else is on this planet that is not intelligent, Prince Derek pushed the frozen Darth Avenger through the portal, ending the terror he had created on Dalmir. Maverick uploaded all the files back on the Starforce computer mainframes restoring all information back, tomorrow will be a brighter day on Dalmir. Vortex looked at Shockwave and said, "It's your turn my friends." He opened another portal to Colvidre, Shockwave, Maverick, Seraph, Rhino, Hightower, and Quill walked through the portal.

Venus found Xamot dead on the infirmary floor, knowing that Dark Avenger had him killed since he was wounded already, Venus bent down next to Xamot and replied, "I am sorry my friend."

Vortex opened another portal to Wildwood, a planet full of tree's, a beautiful planet, not too far from Dalmir the Diamond Enforcers join forces with Starforce on a few occasions, the last time the two joined forces was to save King Melach from his evil brother King Chalem, he said, "Drifter, this portal leads to planet Wildwood, home of the Diamond Enforcers." Drifter put his right hand out to shake his brother's hand, "Thank you, brother. I am eternally grateful for everything you have done, and if you ever need anything I am here for you I owe you one, I will see you again sometime." He disappeared through the portal. Firestar looked around and it seems like everything is going to be back to normal.

On planet Rudsfor a planet protecting one of four powerful diamonds, there is a cyborg on duty always protecting the diamond, inside a crystal temple. The Diamond Enforcers help the cyborgs protect the diamonds from getting in the hands of evil men. Many men surround the temple, the leader of the army is a white wolf named Wolfman. On his right side was a man named Visionary, on his left side was the commander of his army, Commander Zimms, Wolfman said, "Attack! I want that diamond."

To be continued.

THE REIGN OF HELLFIRE

CHAPTER
TWENTY

The sun began to peak over the horizons of a brand-new day, the orange and red colors lit up the sky on Colvidre, Kyle got a message from Commissioner Daniels, *"Officer Young found a recruit for your team, his name is Bullseye. He said he is here to assist Seraph, he keeps talking about a great evil, the dark one."*

Shockwave sat down on his favorite recliner, propped his feet up on the footrest, and thought, *"What a couple of weeks it has been, I would have never thought I would have done all this, if someone would have told me about a month ago. I am not sure if it can get any weirder than this."*

At that very moment there was a knock on the door, as the door opens upstanding at the entrance is Seraph and Hightower as they walked through the entrance. Seraph said, "Hellfire is making his move, we need your help, his plan is to lead a demonic attack on Colvidre to destroy it."

Surprised by the visit Shockwave replied, "I shouldn't be surprised that you two are here, but I am. Commissioner Daniels left me a message saying they found a guy named Bullseye." As he was finishing the sentence, Seraph interrupted him, "Bullseye, he is a friend of mine, also an alien with wings. He must have been sent to help us; he is under the command of a great warrior for my King." Shockwave replied, "It is time to get the team together."

Northstar walked up to Crystal, "I am going to Colvidre, do you want to assist me?" Crystal answered, "I would love to." Northstar replied, "We need to let King Melach know."

As Crystal entered the throne room, she lowered her head to show respect to her King, "My King, Northstar and I are going to Colvidre." Sitting next to the King is his son Prince Derek, "Father, I need to also go, I have spare Starforce communicators for Shockwave and his team to officially assign them as Starforce officers, I will take Firestar and Storm Shadow to protect me."

King Melach acknowledged the request, "Be careful, I don't want to lose you like I lost your mother." Prince Derek jumped up from his seat and charged out of the throne room like a little child, he was so excited to get his team together.

A few minutes later inside the Communication room, Northstar said, "Vortex, get a portal ready for Colvidre." He replied, "It is ready and opening." Northstar, Crystal, Prince Derek, and Firestar and Storm Shadow entered through the portal, and it closed behind them.

As Kyle stopped his cruiser he said, "Alright guys, we are here, let's go see the commissioner."

As they entered the commissioner's office expecting them, he said, "Thank you for coming as soon as you did, we have this man named Bullseye demanding to talk to Seraph. He also said he was sent here to help defeat the dark one. And Kyle the black demon that killed your partner and fellow officer has finally been spotted, he robed another bank, but he escaped without killing anyone this time. I had tried to keep this from you to avoid any grief, but I have no choice, my men are unable to manage this threat."

Seraph answered, "Don't worry sir, I was sent here to stop him, and that is what we are going to do, and return him home to planet Hymlian."

The Commissioner nodded, "Bullseye is waiting for you guys at the Good Night Sleep Inn located on East Bramer Drive in room 112."

As they walked out of the station Maverick caught a glimpse of Northstar and replied, "Northstar! What are you doing here?" Prince Derek walked up to Maverick and said, "Northstar and Crystal said they were coming to Colvidre, and I have the extra communicators like we had discussed, so we can stay in contact." As he handed the communicators to Kyle he replied, "You and your team are officially Starforce Officers here on Colvidre."

Kyle answered, "It is an honor to be a part of Starforce." Hightower said, "We are on our way to meet up with an old friend, do you want to come with us?"

Prince Derek replied, "No, I must be getting back, my father is probably worried about me, and this is the first time that I have been this far from the palace."

Storm Shadow said, "I am going to stay here on Colvidre, I want to find out if the L.E.A. is still in operation. And if it is, I want to pay them a little visit." He was referring to a government funded cloning program called Lawful Elite Agents of which he had been a part of, in fact he was one of their clones, that they created for the government, it was a secret organization that no one talked about.

Prince Derek nodded and replied, "Okay, Firestar are you coming back with me?"

"Yes sir." He pressed his communicator and said, "Vortex, open the portal we are finished here." Prince Derek and Firestar disappear through the portal, and it closed behind them.

Storm Shadow looked around and said, "I will see you guys around." He disappeared

as he walked away, Shockwave said,
"Crystal, you and Northstar are both
welcome on my team, Let's go speak with
Bullseye."

CHAPTER
TWENTY-ONE

An old, abandoned laboratory now called United building it was formally used by the government funded program named L.E.A. before a scientist rebelled against the program and they moved to a new building on the other side of town. To this day the scientist and the clones he took with him are still in hiding, waiting for the perfect time to destroy the program forever.

Hellfire will lead an army, and make war with the entire parallel universes, he had made this laboratory, his base of operations, with the assistance of Night Stalker who had been sent to help Hellfire on his mission.

Night Stalker is a dark shadowy creature, he walks on all four legs, he normally sneaks into people's houses in the dark to feed their minds with fearful thoughts. When you are alone and it is dark, then you feel an evil presence, but do not see anything, and you start thinking fearful thoughts, also your heart begins to race for no reason, it may be a visit from Night Stalker.

Hellfire said, "Northstar is here on Colvidre, I don't think we will be able to defeat him, Seraph, Bullseye and Hightower alone."

Night Stalker replied, "You should get rid of Northstar's mother, capture her or something like that to get him sidetracked."

Hellfire stopped for a moment and thought, *"How can I get close enough to capture Crystal, Seraph will see me before I could grab her."* He got a brilliant idea and said, "I got it! I could go to the past and capture her, then I will bring her to this time, which would solve most of my problems."

Night Stalker hissed, "Yes, that could work, with Crystal missing, there will be no Northstar, but what if when you come back nothing changes?"

Hellfire answered, "If I can get rid of Northstar, I think you and I can manage Seraph and Bullseye, and if we make enough clones, they could manage Hightower and the rest of Starforce."

Shockwave decided it would be better if the team waited outside, as he and Seraph went inside to talk with Bullseye. As they entered the inn, the young lady at the front desk agreed, "Yes, he checked into room #112."

Maverick got out to stretch his legs and to scout out around the inn when his communicator beeped. Maverick pressed the button, "This is Maverick." A voice came through the communicator, "Maverick, this is Commander Hawk, the computers have detected a portal opened on Colvidre, and it is not a Starforce portal. We actually have never seen a portal like this kind of portal, it is reading as a two-way portal, it leads to the past, and it also leads to Dalmir, I want you to go on this mission, bring Rhino with you, I am opening the portal next to you now."

Northstar pressed his communicator, "Commander Hawk, do you need my help on this mission with Maverick?"

"No, sir. I need you to stay on Colvidre just in case something happens on Colvidre or Dalmir." Maverick and Rhino disappeared through the portal as it closed behind them.

Night Stalker had already begun making the army for Hellfire as ordered, the people he had been using were people that they had kidnapped, he was inserting alien spirits inside the bodies making them obedient to do as he and Hellfire command.

Storm Shadow had been watching through a window and thought, *"This is not the L.E.A. but there is something wrong going on here, as a Starforce officer, I need to check into this."*

Opening the window quietly, he snuck through it without being heard, looking around he slowly moved closer to Night Stalker, crouching and slowly moving closer, until he bumped into a table the noise caught Night Stalkers attention and he looked around and noticed Storm Shadow and he said, "You have no business here, but it is too late now." He motioned for the aliens to take over the bodies, that he had ready for them, and he motioned for them to attack Storm Shadow. About twelve bodies had been prepared for the aliens to take over so far, and after a quick fight the twelve overpowered Storm Shadow, they tied him up to a table and left him for Hellfire to decide what to do with him.

Bullseye had been looking out the window of his hotel room, looking at all the surrounding, he examined the sky, and all the clouds in the sky, he was beginning to miss the brightness of his home world; the sun is closer on his planet, then it is on Colvidre, the heat is also more bearable. Suddenly there was a knock on his door, as he opened the door, he saw a familiar face and said, "Seraph, my friend, I have missed you. Captain Mikael sent me to assist you and to bring you more information. The dark ones (a group of terrorists of his home planet) have sent Night Stalker to aid Hellfire, they are planning to create an army of hosts for the alien parasites to make war on the universes, they are planning to start here on Colvidre." Seraph replied, "Night Stalker, he is a nut job. Good thing they did not bring Brimstone. We can manage Night Stalker and Hellfire the parasite aliens may give us hassle though."

Bullseye added, "They have already started kidnapping people, I saw on the police bulletin board there are already a few people who have gone missing."

In the past on planet Dalmir, a portal opens on a sidewalk next to an empty lot, but in the present time there is a statue of a peace maker, Dax Nucleon who heroically saved Dalmir from going to war against an organization called the rebellion of secret affairs, Hellfire walked out of the portal, his plan is to find Crystal, capture her and take her to the present time, where Northstar will no longer exist.

Hellfire looked at the angle of the sun and determined that it is close to three o'clock in the afternoon on planet Dalmir, Crystal should now be at the Starforce recruit training graduation, today is the day she graduates from a trainee to an official officer, Hellfire wanted to capture her before she became an officer, Hellfire is on his way to the Starforce graduation ceremony.

Another portal opened on the other side of Dalmir closer to the Starforce headquarters, Venus, Maverick, Rhino, and Firestar stepped out of it, Firestar said, "Okay guys, here is what we know, someone teleported here right before us, the person is here for Starforce for some reason, we need to stop this person before our time is compromised by this, and we must not fail, Whatever the plan is, it has to be pure evil."

Hellfire knows where he is going, he has studied Starforce officers and their territories, he knows that the best time to catch Starforce off guard is right when they start the ceremony he thought, *"Starforce officers will be on guard while the king and Prince are on stage, but they will not suspect me to start a distraction at the start of the ceremony."* Hellfire walks close to the ceremony area and looks at the stage and there are quite a few graduates sitting in the seats, but he does not see Crystal yet.

King Aleka and Prince Melach walked out on stage to start the ceremony, Prince Melach sat in the back of the stage while his sentry guard is standing behind him monitoring the crowd, King Aleka said, "Good afternoon Students, this has been a tough training course, but I am impressed by all of the students many have accomplished things no other Starforce officer had the ability to. As this new generation of officers arise, a new generation of evil also arises, we must all adapt to the coming age."

As Hellfire walked through the crowd, his appearance caught the attention of King Aleka's Sentry guard speaking through his communicator, "All officers be on guard, there is a strange guy walking through the crowd of people."

Hellfire noticed the heightened security and knew he needed a distraction, so he shot King Aleka using his hellish body parts, one of the students ran up to Hellfire, out of his back he shot out a big black splinter, hitting the student and killing him instantly, another student ran to the fallen officer's side, "Kahl don't die." Hellfire looked back at the student and laughed, one of those laughs that would send an eerie feeling through your body, seeing Crystal he turned around and grabbed her, opening a portal he drags her through it, and the portal closed behind them.

As the portal closed, everything stood still including time itself, life as everyone knew was now gone. A portal opened next to Firestar, with fierce winds blowing around the portal it sucked Maverick, Venus, Rhino, and Firestar through the portal as it slammed shut.

CHAPTER TWENTY-TWO

Forget everything that you have just read or have heard, everything has changed, the world known as reality is now gone thanks to Hellfire. It only took one person to destroy a world that everyone built. Hellfire did want to get rid of Northstar, but what he did not plan is what will happen to the world, after he destroyed the past by capturing Crystal, before she had graduated Starforce training, all this just to get rid of one person.

A portal opened and out of the portal came Hellfire and Crystal, she was struggling trying to break free from the grips of Hellfire, unable to free herself since Hellfire is too strong, after a brief struggle he knocked her out, so that he didn't have to continue to fight her, Hellfire didn't know that this world was different from the world he came from.

Another portal opened on Colvidre fierce winds blew out of this portal, throwing Venus, Maverick, Rhino and Firestar out of it as it slammed shut, a blast of light was left where the portal had closed. Rhino looked around and he noticed a few things that he had recognized and asked, "We are home, how did this happen?" With a dreadful look on his face Venus answered, "We have failed, and something had been changed for us to be thrown out of the portal, I wonder what he changed in the past to create this world, and what has changed in this world." Maverick pressed his communicator, "Starforce, this is Maverick."

A voice from the speaker of the communicator said, "Maverick who? How did you manage to get a Starforce communicator?" Firestar pressed his communicator, "This is Firestar." The voice echoed over the communicator, "Firestar, this is Commander Hawk, we had thought something had happened to you, we had been unable to get in contact with you, have you found Drifter?" Firestar answered, "Why would I be looking for Drifter? We were sent by Prince Derek to save Starforce in the past."

Commander Hawk said, "Drifter escaped prison here on Dalmir and was spotted in Colvidre, your mission was to find Drifter and capture him, never address our King as a Prince. Now get back to your mission, and do not contact me again until Drifter has been captured."

Rhino said, "I don't understand this, Drifter was never sent to prison, he was just helping us and joined forces with the Diamond Enforcers." Venus spoke up, "We are not in our world, we are in a world created by the same person, who we were sent to the past to stop, we failed and now we must find out what he did to change our world to this world."

Firestar replied, "Prince Derek is our King in this world." Maverick said, "And I am not a Starforce officer in this world, we need to find Shockwave." Rhino answered, "I hope things haven't changed too badly, and I hope we can fix this, so we can get back to our world."

In this world, Crystal never came to Colvidre, Hellfire killed Kahl at the Starforce graduation ceremony, the Dark Avenger was still going by his Starforce name Spartan, he has not betrayed Starforce yet since Kahl is not here to assist him, he is still an active Starforce Officer, Quill was charged for the murder of his parents. Hightower was hired to represent him as his attorney, he has won every case to which he was assigned to, until this case, he had lost it, since he had no proof that Quill did not kill his parents, he became so angry that he grew tall and destroyed an abandoned warehouse, as the police arrived, they arrested him. Shockwave was convicted of destroying police records, he was sent to prison, which is where he met Quill and Hightower, Shockwave knowing Quill's father James, he came up with a plan to escape prison so they could find out who framed them. Commander Jurgon realized how dangerous people could be, and if they could control their superpowers they would become even more dangerous, he then created a group of police officers that he named the Enforcers, they have the authority to arrest and/or kill people who exhibit unusual powers that he does not understand. Tritan had never turned evil, he is still a very smart scientist, he also created his own team which he calls them the Outlanders, he gives people what they want and that is power, but in return he teaches them how to use and control the powers bestowed on them, with his assistant Rex, one of his students was a man named Kevin Fitzwater, he wanted power to help the police catch a criminal who killed his family, but the police would not help him, he now has the ability to generate, manipulate, and project ice with Tritan's help he will be able to learn how to use his powers, since he currently cannot control his powers, which has earned him the name Blizzard.

In the distant future of this reality on Dalmir inside Starforce headquarters, sitting on the throne is King Derek's son King Zimein, Northstar is in his presence requesting to be allowed to save the past from Hellfire in hopes of ending his reign of terror once and for all, Northstar said, "My King, Hellfire has been a threat to Dalmir and the surrounding systems and planets, as we all know Hellfire destroyed the past by kidnapping my mother from her time and taking her to another time, creating this reality that we now live. I believe it is possible to destroy Hellfire and take my mother back to her original time and restore reality and end Hellfire's reign of terror." King Zimein replied, "What if you are wrong? What if his reign exists after reality is restored? Or what if you fail?" Northstar replied, "That is a chance I must take."

This is a dark future where all kinds of creatures of the day and night roam the worlds by the command of Hellfire.

Lance Batt the king's holy man and faithful advisor spoke up, "My King, I will go with Northstar and assist him, when he faces Hellfire, he will be up against the darkest evil known to all worlds, the prince of darkness must be stopped at any cost." One of the King's sentry guards said, "Your Majesty, the headquarters is under attack by an unknown force. They might be following the orders of Hellfire or King Chazlek." He answered, "Alright, send all my sentry guards and all remaining officers to face this attack, soon as I am done here, I will lead the defense. Northstar, you and Lance make sure Hellfire's reign of terror never happens, go to the teleporting computer. Take this identifying teleporting card have the machine scan the card and Dival will make sure you are teleported to the correct time."

Starforce is more advance and more powerful in this future. Northstar wears a black armor which makes him almost invincible, in the middle of his chest is the Starforce symbol, a symbol of justice and truth. Northstar is more of a threat now then he was before, Lance wears a black armor with a white collar to signify set apart to holy things, located at the top left corner of his armor, above his heart is where his Starforce symbol is located at, these two warriors are more then what Hellfire bargained for. A portal was opened by Dival the teleporting artificial intelligence

Northstar and Lance disappeared through the portal as it closed behind them.

CHAPTER TWENTY-THREE

On Colvidre present time, Crystal woke up and hit Hellfire in the nose, a distraction that gave her the chance to make an escape from him. She got a few blocks away before he knew she had escaped. Hellfire thought, *"I did it! I will not be bother by Northstar, now I just need to find Night Stalker."* Hellfire disappeared, and his evil laugh was heard for miles.

The portal opened and Northstar walked out from the portal, "The sun, and blue sky, what a beautiful sight to behold." Before he had finished speaking, Lance stepped out of the portal and it closed behind him, he replied, "This is what a world looks like where Hellfire doesn't rule."

At Starforce headquarters Commander Hawk said to King Derek, "Your Majesty, we have received warning of another portal opening up on Colvidre, that makes three portals in one day, but this last portal is showing up as a two-way portal." King Derek replied, "I want you to go to Colvidre, and investigate these portals take Spartan with you." He nodded.

Maverick left Venus, Rhino and Firestar outside as he walked in the Colvidre Police department, As he walked in the doors he glanced around and he could tell a lot has changed, the place use to be well kept and clean, but as he looked around there was clutter everywhere, you could tell that no one cleaned the building anymore, walking up to the information desk he replied, "Is Detective Blake here?" Her gruff voice echoed, "Sorry sir, there is no one with that name employed here, but I do know who you are looking for. He was kicked off the force and arrested until he escaped prison and now, he is considered armed and dangerous, so if you do find him, please give us a call, he is an extremely dangerous man." As Maverick turned around and started walking towards the front door, he wanted to wash his hands of the filth that was on the front desk, but the front door and glass windows were just as bad. As he walked back to where the guys were standing, he said, "It is worse than we originally thought, he is considered an escaped criminal on the run, I wonder who the good guys in town are if he is a bad guy." Rhino replied, "I cannot believe this, we must find him and get to the bottom of this world." Firestar answered, "Yes, I agree. We must find the underlying cause of what has changed." A guy walking past had ease dropped on parts of the conversation, he walked up to them and said, "If your friend is lost, there is a superhero team that might be able to help you in your search, they are really good at finding people, they are about five blocks south down this road, the building is on the right side of the road, and they are inside a building that has neon paint on the building that says *UNITED,* you guys should check it out they may be able to help you, or point you in the right direction." Rhino answered, "Sounds like something Shockwave would do." The four of them left and started heading south towards the building painted United.

Another portal opened, and Commander Hawk and Spartan stepped out of the portal as it closed behind them, Commander Hawk said, "We must regroup with the Starforce officers here, they are just down the road."

Spartan looked around and saw a lady looking suspicious and acting strange, "Commander, look over there, that lady is acting strange, I think she may need help." Crystal had gotten tired of running, but she continued looking over her shoulder, she had known that she had lost Hellfire, so she stopped to catch her breath. As she looked around, she did not see anything that looked familiar, a guy walked past her and she stopped him, "Excuse me." As he stopped, she continued, "Do you know where I can find Starforce?" The guy looked at her strange and said, "Starforce? They are forbidden here on Colvidre." He continued to walk away from her, it was as if the name Starforce was forbidden to say on Colvidre.

Spartan walked up to her and said, "Who are you? And how do you know about Starforce?" Crystal replied, "My name is Crystal, and the last thing I remember is going to my Starforce graduation, but getting kidnapped by some creature in black, I need to make my way back to Starforce, so that I can graduate and become a Starforce officer." Spartan answered, "I remember something like that happening about twenty years ago, and a friend of mine named Kahl was murdered that day." Shockingly Crystal replied, "Twenty years ago? No, this just happened yesterday, it was not that long ago, I must get back to Starforce, can you help me?" Commander Hawk said, "We are on a mission right now, and as you have heard Starforce is forbidden here on Colvidre, so this is a stealthy mission, but after we are finished with our mission, we will take you back with us to Starforce headquarters." Crystal was relieved, "Thank you, sir."

Inside the building painted *UNITED*, Tritan said, "Rex, there was a special news update on television earlier, they said that there were two guys who appeared from a portal, and the Colvidre police are on high alert to find them, I need you to go find them before the police find them, I believe they are from Starforce, and you know what they symbol looks like." Rex nodded, "Yes, boss, I will find them."

Firestar saw Rex as he was leaving the building, "I will follow this guy, he looks suspicious, Maverick, you Venus and Rhino check this place out." Maverick knocked on the entrance to the building, Blizzard opened the door, revealing Tritan in the background, "Tritan! Where is Shockwave?" I do not know who you are talking about, but you guys can come in and I will help you in your search." Rhino tapped Maverick's shoulder, "Come on guys. We do not need to fight Tritan; he is not the reason we are here." As they turned away from the building, they saw Seraph and Bullseye, "Let's follow Seraph, maybe he will lead us to Shockwave." Maverick agreed with Venus.

Inside a secret building, a building that Shockwave calls his special forces building, Shockwave said, "Guys, I can't figure out who would frame us." While he was speaking the door opened, standing at the entrance is Seraph, "I am Seraph, and this is my friend Bullseye, we are on a special mission and we need your help, the fate of the world is at risk."

Shockwave invited them inside, "We will help you." Maverick was standing not too far from Seraph, and he saw Shockwave, "Shockwave, I am Maverick, this is Venus and Rhino." Rhino was relieved to see Shockwave, "We have been looking for you, we need your help. There is a great evil, and he is trying to destroy everything." Maverick replied, "Shockwave, you may not know us, but we know you, your name is Kyle Blake, you had worked with the Colvidre police, as a Detective, Rhino and I are a part of your team." Shockwave looked around at all the guys and answered, "I don't know any of you guys, and this is the only team I am a part of." Bullseye said, "Hellfire is destroying your world, we must stop him from succeeding, he already has turned our world into a strange world. Hellfire is the prince of an evil group from my world called Darkness hunters, he was sent to Colvidre to create havoc and to destroy everything, Seraph and I are here to stop him." Venus replied, "In our world, we were sent to stop Hellfire, but we don't know any of his plan, and so we failed, and he created this reality." Shockwave interrupted, "We are wasting time here, if we are going to stop him, we are going to need more help, Let's go ask Tritan, for his assistance." Maverick said, "Tritan is a bad guy, why would he help us?" Shockwave was surprised at Maverick, "Tritan is not a bad guy, he is a member of my team, and he will want to be a part of this." They left for the building called *United* where Tritan has set up his headquarters.

On the streets Northstar and Lance were searching for Hellfire and Crystal, when Rex walked up to them, "Are you two lost?" Northstar replied, "No, we are looking for someone." Rex said, "I see your Starforce symbol on your chests, my master sent me to find you two, and bring you guys to him, his name is Tritan." Northstar looked around and the streets were empty, "Tritan, I remember hearing about him, he was a protector of Colvidre with the assistance of Shockwave, we will follow you to Tritan."

Firestar watched Rex as he was talking to the Starforce officers, and he almost recognized Northstar, the armor that he wore made him unsure, he had never seen Northstar wear an armor, the other guy didn't even look close to anyone he knew. Firestar pressed his communicator, "Are there any Starforce officers currently on Colvidre, if so head towards the building called *UNITED*, I have encountered someone who resembles Northstar, and he may need our help." The communicator started beeping, "Firestar, this is Commander Hawk, my team is on our way."

CHAPTER
TWENTY-FOUR

Hellfire finally arrived at his headquarters called *UNITED*, not knowing the reality has changed, trying to open the door he noticed it was locked, he knocked, "Night Stalker, let me in the door." Tritan opened the door, "Can I help you?" "Tritan! What are you doing here? And where is Night Stalker?" Tritan looked behind Hellfire and all around, "Do I know you?" Hellfire pushed Tritan out of the way, to make his way in the building, "Are you going to help me destroy this world?" Tritan punched Hellfire in the face and said, "No, I will not help you, I will stop you." Hellfire shot some black sharp pieces out of his hands, hitting Tritan and knocking him to the ground, "You are a weak fool, you had the chance to join me and become a master of this reality." As Tritan took his last few breaths, he said, "You will never defeat all of my team, and wait until Starforce shows up." Blizzard hearing all the commotion walks in the room, he ran to Tritan and said, "Tritan, stay with us, I will get the others." Shockwave and his team walk through the door, Seraph exclaims, "Hellfire is here." As they all hurried inside

the building they found Tritan laying on the
floor dead, Blizzard snuck up to Hellfire and
said, "You killed my teacher, that will be the
last mistake you will ever have the chance
to make, you will die." He punched Hellfire
in the gut, Rex walked in the building
looking around and he saw Blizzard punch
Hellfire and said, "What is happening here?
Where is Tritan?" Shockwave pointed to the
body covered in blood and laying on the
floor lifeless. Northstar followed Rex
through the building and screamed,
"HELLFIRE!" Hellfire looks back at Northstar,
"You're alive, my plan has failed." Hellfire
looks around the building and is surrounded
by heroes circling around him, ready to give
their lives for this world and all the people
in this world. Crystal and Spartan walked in
the building, and she pointed at Hellfire,
"That is the evil man who kidnapped me,
and brought me to the strange world."
Hellfire laughed as he was getting very
angry, "Attack me if you dare." Venus shot
an energy blast at Hellfire, as he did, Hellfire
blocked the hit, then he shot black objects
out of his hands, hitting Firestar, Rex, and
Shockwave knocking them to the ground,

with such a jolt that it knocked them out cold. Blizzard ran back up to Hellfire and he shot a few icicles at him, but they melted before they got close enough to him, Hellfire shot a blast of fire at Blizzard knocking him back towards the ground, Quill came down the stairs and shot a few quills out of his body, aiming for Hellfire, but before the quills even left his body Hellfire dodged them. One quill hit Spartan in the leg, another hit Commander Hawk, and Maverick flew in the air to dodge the other two. Hellfire shot another blast of fire; this time he aimed for Quill, the blast hit him, knocking him to the ground. Venus used this distraction as an advantage to get close enough to Hellfire, so that he could shot another energy blast at him, it hit him, knocking him into the wall on the other side of the building.

As he managed to get up from that hit, he began to laugh, the evil laugh echoed all throughout the building, sending chill bumps down the spines of everyone that heard it. Hellfire blasted some of those sharp black objects out of his chest, hitting

Venus knocking him to the ground, Rhino ducked his head pointing his horn at Hellfire and started running towards Hellfire, but he punched him, making his Rhino skinned body fly through the air, the weight of his body when it hit the ground, his landing shakes the foundations of the building.

Hellfire stood up and looked around the building he noticed that all the heroes were either standing or getting up from the ground, besides the casualties, he saw through their eyes, into their hearts, and he realized that they were ready to fight to the death, Lance took this opportunity to fly above Hellfire to get himself to the back side of Hellfire, when he landed on the other side of Hellfire, Northstar fired a laser gun hitting Hellfire knocking him down to the ground, that hit made him so mad that he made his wings come out of his back, his wings are black, and sharp, very evil looking, Lance went up to Hellfire a desperate move but one that Lance had determined to make, he grabbed him and pulled out his laser pistol, firing it at Hellfire as he held him tight, electrocuting Lance as well as Hellfire. They both fell to the ground, Lance could barely breathe, his breathing continued to slow down, Northstar ran up to Lance, "I did this for our world and everyone in it, and now maybe they will be able to see the sky, the way I was able to see it today, forgive me. Cough...Cough." Northstar replied, "You will be remembered as the hero who defeated the greatest evil the world has ever known, goodbye my friend." As he finished speaking Lance died. Northstar turned his gaze at Hellfire, who was trying to crawl away, unable to stand on his feet, Northstar looked up and Seraph was standing in front of Hellfire preventing his escape, Hellfire looked up and saw his exit was blocked by Seraph, so he turned the other way to see Shockwave stood up and moved to block him. All of a sudden, a portal opened and the room lit up as bright as the sun, a figure was seen inside the portal holding a fiery sword his wings was spread wide, the figure bent down and grabbed Hellfire, picking him up by his collar bone, as he did they disappeared through the portal, it closed behind them taking the bright light along with it. Standing where Hellfire had just been, Seraph said, "Thank you, my friends, you all have helped defeat an evil this world does not need to face." Northstar replied, "What about Lance?" Bullseye answered, "I am sorry. He did make the right choice; he died a hero." Shockwave inquired, "Who was the angel in the portal with the fiery sword?" Seraph answered, "That is Mikal, our commander officer." Bullseye looked around the room, "Our time is up here, we get to go home. Our mission is finally over." They both said their goodbyes to the team and disappeared.

Crystal feeling out of place, "I want to go home, I still need to graduate Starforce." Commander Hawk replied, "I will take care of that." Pressing his communicator he continued, "Open a portal from Colvidre to Dalmir, twenty years in the past." A voice echoed from the communicator, "It will take me a few minutes to get the coordinates correct." A few minutes later, the portal opened, Commander Hawk, Spartan, Maverick, and Quill escorted Crystal through the portal, to take her to

her correct time in hopes of fixing the
present time by stopping Hellfire.

CHAPTER
TWENTY-FIVE

The portal opened twenty years in the past, near the Starforce headquarters, where the graduation ceremony takes place, as they stepped out of the portal it closed behind them. Maverick spotted Hellfire walking towards the graduation center of Starforce headquarters, Commander Hawk said, "Crystal, wait here. Spartan stay with her and guard her with your life, Maverick, Quill and myself will go and stop Hellfire." "Yes, sir." Spartan replied. Maverick continued to keep his attention on Hellfire and said, "Do you have a plan on how we are going to stop Hellfire? We failed the last time." Commander Hawk answered, "All we have to do is make sure he does not kill anyone of this time, and as soon as he captures Crystal, he will teleport out of here, and then we will replace Crystal with our Crystal." Quill said, "I don't think that will work. If we do that, we will have two Crystal's in our timeline, and nothing would have changed. But then again if we save both Crystal's there will be two Crystal's in this timeline."

Hellfire walked closer to Commander Hawk; he was looking confused like he wasn't sure where he was going, and no one was around. Quill yelled, "Hellfire, your reign of terror ends today!" Hellfire jerked his head and said, "You guys are more resourceful than I had originally thought, I have underestimated you, but it will not happen again, I promise you that." Commander Hawk was frustrated that Quill didn't keep his mouth shut, "Great, we don't need this. If we are seen by any of the other Starforce officers, it will be possible that the future will change again, we need to be careful." Quill shot out a quill needle from the tip of his Ponting finger, he was aiming at Hellfire, but he dodged the quill. Hellfire replied, "I don't know how you guys found me so fast, but it doesn't really matter, because I will end this now." As he was talking, he shot out black sharp objects again out from his skin, Maverick flew up in the air so he could dodge the objects, he shot a blast of energy out of his fists, hitting Hellfire in the ribs, knocking him to the ground. As Hellfire gained his footing he stood back up, and he spotted Spartan and Crystal behind

Commander Hawk. He laughed as he opened a portal and entered through it, the other end opened next to Crystal, he stepped out of the portal long enough to grab Crystal and dragged her back through the portal.

Quill replied, "Alright, we did it, our time should have changed back to normal." Another portal opened, and strong winds came out of the portal as the guys got sucked back through the portal.

The sun rises on another day on Colvidre as normal, Shockwave has his own Starforce headquarters on Colvidre thanks to Prince Derek. He and his team stay in contact with both the Police and Starforce daily. Colvidre's Starforce officers consist of Shockwave, Crystal, Northstar, Rhino, Quill and Maverick. This world hasn't changed a lot, and it is what they call home. There is a knock on the door, it is Seraph, and he says, "Shockwave, I need you and your team once again, my mission is not over yet."

Elsewhere in the shadows between two tall buildings, two red glowing eyes appear and an evil laugh is heard throughout the whole town, the kind of laugh that when you hear it, it sends chill bumps up and down your spine. A shadowy figure steps out of the dark and says, "Tritan, I will have my revenge on you."

Epilogue

Kyle looked around and he was standing in a valley full of grass, he continued to look around and all he could see around himself was the valley, he looked up to the sky and it looked like a normal sky, as he moved his gaze back to eye level, he saw a mysterious man appear out of thin air. The man said, "Kyle, my name is Kailak I am your father." Surprised he replied, "My father? How can this be, you died long before I could remember." Kailak answered, "It was a sad day when I sent you and your mother in to hiding, but I had no choice I had to save your life." My father Savante wanted my royal bloodline destroyed. My son you are royalty, don't let my sacrifice be in vain. It is time for you to rise and take the throne, that you are destined to rule on." With a jolt Kyle woke up and said, "What a strange dream."

For more information on the Author or any of his other work or other illustrations, visit **amazon.com/author/jeremyhoward**

You can also like the adventures of Starforce facebook page, and stay up to date with all the adventures of Starforce